Tamzin Clarke

v

the Mummy

Lauren and Robert Stock

For Robert Paul and Robert Edward
Father and Grandfathers
Both have taken the final journey
We wish them adventures untold

1

"You were what?"

"I was murdered."

My hands were shaking, and I felt light headed. *Murdered*? I couldn't believe this—it couldn't be happening. "What? Why didn't you tell me before? Who killed you?"

I was talking to Daniel, a new friend who had saved my life more than once as we battled Jack the Ripper. And if you couldn't tell from our conversation... Yeah, he was a ghost.

"I really don't know, Tamzin. When I first saw you and spoke to you, I didn't want you to know that I was different. After that, my feelings for you just got stronger. I was worried it might make our weird relationship even weirder."

"And you really don't know what happened or who did it?"

"I've thought about it a lot, but it's like there's something missing, something that I can't remember for the life of me," he said, sighing. Then he chuckled. "No pun intended... I think I remember being here, at the shore, on the day it happened, but that's my last real memory of being alive."

"Did someone want to kill you? Were you involved in anything sketchy?"

"No, not that I recall. But hey, can we just sit here and relax and try not to think about this now? Bringing Vickie back was harder than expected, and I need to rest."

"Okay... Thank you so much for doing that. I don't know if I would've been able to move on otherwise."

Vickie had been killed by Jack the Ripper. We finally defeated him by sending him back to his dark dimension, but Vickie and Daniel had been sucked into the vortex as well. I was worried that they would be stuck there forever.

I was still holding Daniel close, and now I squeezed him even tighter and put my head on his shoulder. I didn't want to let him go, but I could tell that he was exhausted. We both sat down, and I snuggled up next to him. After a few minutes, we laid down together. My hand found his.

"Uhm..." I half whispered. "When you were fighting the Ripper in the tunnel... You said you were in love with me?" I said it as a question, even though I knew that was exactly what he had said.

Without hesitation, he said, "Yes."

I hoped he would say something else so I didn't have to respond. I didn't really know what to say. I squeezed his hand, and he stroked mine with his thumb. I waited a few moments, and he finally spoke up.

"You are an amazing person. I've had a few girlfriends, but you... You are so much more."

"So much more what?"

"Lots of things. You're beautiful. You're strong. Your smile can cheer me up no matter what is happening in our lives." He looked over at me.

"Oh, wow." I blushed and turned my head away, looking at the sky.

"Whenever you see me, I mean, other than when we're running for our lives, your smile is just so... I don't know, it feels so genuine—like you're actually happy to see me."

"Anything else?" I asked. I was joking around at this point. I wasn't really expecting anything seeing as he had already said so much.

"You are loyal—you wouldn't leave Maxie to her fate with Jack, even if it meant putting your life in danger. You're one of the smartest girls I've known... Actually, you *are* the smartest."

"Wow, Daniel, I don't even know what to say. Thank you." He looked at me sidelong, and I directed my gaze down at our entwined hands. I pushed a piece of hair out of my face, adjusting my position slightly. I could feel his gaze on me, but I didn't feel embarrassed. If anything I felt more confident. I wanted him to look at me like I was the only girl that really mattered because, in that moment, it felt like the truth.

Daniel yawned. For a second, I was confused—do ghosts yawn? Then I remembered how drained he was and figured it didn't really matter. I turned my body into his, putting my hand on his chest. After a few minutes, we both fell asleep.

2

I was helping out at my dad's antique shop today. Clarke's Antiques was receiving a shipment from an Egyptian dealer—although my dad said he was more of a smuggler. Apparently, the current shipment was going to be reunited with other items from the pyramid excavation exhibit in our local science museum. Dad seemed to be excited about the *Mummy Extravaganza*, as it was called. He'd been spending a lot of time at the hospital visiting Mom, so I think having something else to focus his attention on sparked his enthusiasm.

I was dusting off the showroom tables when the front door swung open.

"Delivery for Thomas Clarke."

A young delivery woman pushed a hand truck with some shipping crates.

"Hello," I said. "I can sign for them."

"Here," she said, handing me the bill of lading. She gave me a pen and pointed, and I signed.

"Where would you like the crates?"

"Uhm... I have to open them in the back room."

"Ah, okay. I will truck them back there for you. I've delivered to your dad before."

"Thank you!" I said as we maneuvered to the back. I held the curtain open, and she expertly pushed the truck around the remaining obstacles.

"No problem," she said. "I hope your mom gets out of the hospital soon."

"Yeah, me too."

"It was all over the news about the police station being attacked. She was lucky. My uncle was a cop—he was killed..." She hung her head for a moment, a fleeting sad expression crossing her face, then she looked up at me.

"I'm very sorry to hear about your uncle. My mom was incredibly lucky. *Angel Jack* was insane."

She nodded. "All of that was definitely crazy... All right, I need to get back to delivering."

I waved as she headed toward the front door. I inspected the boxes—they definitely looked like they had been shipped from overseas. The wooden exteriors were dingy and covered with scratches and dirt smudges.

I called the back room of the antique store the *Dungeon of Curious Oddities*. It was where we stored items before putting them on the showroom floor or getting them to my dad's private clients.

The hairs on the back of my neck suddenly stood on end. I had the strangest feeling that I was being watched... I turned around to see the antique doll on the shelf staring directly at me. God, she was creepy.

Two of the containers that had been shipped were cubes that could have held a large toaster, the third was twice as wide and a bit taller. I pulled down the topmost crate, grabbed a small crowbar, and carefully started removing the nails that held the wooden panels together. Pulling off the top piece of wood, a wad of paper stuffing popped up. Carefully moving aside the packing revealed a stone tablet with some kind of hieroglyphic inscription on it. Assuming the tablet was from ancient Egypt, it seemed well preserved. I guessed that it must have been in a burial chamber that had been excavated recently.

The next box went pretty much the same way. Moving aside the paper stuffing, a face looked back at me. I jumped, not expecting that, but then moved in closer. The face was actually a mask—a mask of a flawless female. The bejeweled eyes were the only things that were not in a purely human vein. In all honesty, I was mesmerized by the face. She was beautiful, almost hypnotically so.

The final box opened quickly. Pulling away the stuffing, I was hit with a blast of light. My eyes squeezed shut with the intensity. I wasn't sure where the light was coming from, but it must have been directly reflecting off the metal. Once my eyes adjusted, I realized that inside the box was a golden scepter in the form of an ankh. The edges of the ankh had multi-colored jewels. This piece also seemed to be pristine. "Pick me up," it seemed to say. Before I could even think about it, my hand was reaching in toward it. *What?* I pulled back, not wanting to be drawn to this thing for reasons out of my control. After battling a demonic Jack the Ripper, I wasn't sure what other paranormal stuff existed in our world.

Stepping back further, I remembered the scarab beetle brooch my dad had received a few weeks ago. The Ripper had been interested in it, but I wasn't sure what he was going to do with it. I walked over to the shelf, thankfully nowhere near that antique doll, where the gold inlaid box sat, and I opened it. The scarab was covered in rubies and other stones. Unlike the ankh, the scarab didn't compel me to pick it up. The instinct was there, though, and I grabbed it to put it on. It had a fastener that I wasn't familiar with, but I secured it onto my shirt easily enough. I wasn't really sure why I was fascinated with the bug—it just felt *right*.

Looking in one of the mirrors, the scarab almost looked like a pet hanging onto me. After all of my encounters with dragonflies, I wasn't as creeped out by having an insect on my shirt as I normally would have been. When I saw it begin to move and crawl over my heart, I should have screamed. Instead, I couldn't take my eyes off of it. I barely felt the sting as it bit into my skin. My last thought as I fainted was hoping that I didn't crush the bug when I hit the floor.

I was standing on a large balcony looking out over a sea of people. "Amenhotep… Amenhotep…" They shouted in unison.

The people were in a huge courtyard, stone statues sitting atop high walls that surrounded them. The statues depicted ancient pharaohs or gods looking down upon the masses as if the people were ants. The walls were intricately carved, featuring busts interspersed with colorful frescoes.

The air was acrid and hot, and my lips and tongue were parched. I desperately wanted a glass of water, but somehow knew that I had to wait here.

There was a young man standing near me. He had some kind of headpiece—ornate gold hanging down beside his ears with a ceremonial scarab sitting front and center. Both his head and face were clean shaven. His linen robes were white with adornments of red and black, and he had leather sandals that climbed up his ankles.

I tried to look further on either side but could only swivel my head part of the way around. I was startled when I turned, or more correctly, the body I was on turned toward the young man. I had no control over my movements, but I could now look behind him to see a huge curtained entrance leading to a chamber.

On the other side of the young man (boy?) was a girl. She was a teenager wearing a beautiful robe and headdress. The symbol on her headpiece was an ankh, reminding me of the ankh scepter in the shipping crate. Her hair was jet black and hung in a braid down her back.

The boy waved out over the crowd and they chanted even louder. Giant pillars lined the walls of the courtyard. There was another building toward the back wall with a large arch over a road leading to a city of mud brick homes. From our high perch, I was able to see that some of the roofs were open over courtyards of their own. Off in the distance was a pyramid surrounded by some type of scaffolding.

The girl was smiling at the boy as he waved. I don't know why, but something about that smile made me upset. The boy turned and walked back toward the curtain and the girl's eyes looked directly above me. Her smile disintegrated and her eyes went cold. I felt something like panic, and then the girl followed the boy. There were two guards standing on either side of the curtain, and I was suddenly moving between them.

As I entered the inner chamber, I spied a brass disc on the wall. It was highly polished and I could see a girl trailing the young couple. I gasped when I saw the scarab brooch on her robe. As she moved into the room, I realized that I was seeing things from the perspective of her scarab pin...

The couple had stopped outside of heavy wooden double doors and were talking. My girl was wearing a much simpler robe, so I surmised that she must have been some kind of servant. Further, *since she had the scarab which matched the boy's, I thought she might be his servant.*

I looked at the boy and suddenly felt a tightness in my stomach. In a flash, I sensed that he was the prince, son of Amenhotep, and that he was to marry the girl who was the high priestess. I did not like her...

When these thoughts and feelings arose I understood that they came from the servant girl. The scarab brooch connected us somehow.

The prince smiled at me, my heart skipping a few beats. He waved, then opened the wooden doors and entered what seemed to be bed chambers. There were hanging fabrics surrounding a massive bed in the center of the room. A pool was off to the left and a side table and bench were on the right. He entered the room with the priestess following. She turned around to close the doors—her eyes caught mine. At first, they narrowed. Then she flashed a wicked smile in my direction and winked.

My entire being was overcome with emotion. I was angry—I was crushed—I was defeated. I loved him... and she was just using him.

~

I bolted upright. What the hell was that? It was much more vivid than a dream. Was it some kind of vision?

I looked down at the scarab. It seemed to be pleading, "I didn't do anything." It was in its original position where I had fastened it, and there was no sign of broken skin where I had sworn it had bitten me. Weird...

I got back to uncrating the items, making sure not to touch the ankh scepter. When I was done, I locked up the showroom and went up to make dinner for me and Dad. He should be home from visiting Mom at the hospital soon, and I wanted to do something special for him. Time to bake up some beef and cheese stuffed manicotti!

~

8

I heard the door open and hopped off the couch. For whatever reason, I was extra happy to see my dad. Maybe it had something to do with the vision?

"Hey, Dad."

"Hey, Sweetie. I smell something good."

"I managed to make stuffed manicotti all by myself."

"Without your assistant?"

"Yep," I said, smiling and sticking my tongue out.

He gave me a big hug, and we proceeded to the kitchen. There was still time before it was done, so we sat down at the table.

"How was Mom today?"

"Good. She's getting stronger every day. The doctors are still not sure on when they will release her, but her healing continues."

"I am going to stay with her for a few hours tomorrow."

"She will appreciate that," Dad said. He leaned back, shoulders slumping. The strain of having Mom in the hospital was wearing on him.

"A shipment arrived today," I said, hoping to change the subject. It seemed to make him a little happier.

"Excellent! Which one was it?"

"The artifacts from that Egyptian guy. The one you said was pretty much a smuggler."

"Oh, very nice! The museum will be happy to hear it. Those items had disappeared from the excavated tomb and had held up the *Mummy Extravaganza* exhibit."

My dad suddenly sat up straight and grinned.

"What?" I asked.

"The museum curator for the antiquities is an old friend. I haven't seen her for many years."

"Wow, small world. I think it'll be good for you to see an old friend. Maybe take your mind off of all the recent craziness."

"Her name is Miral. I knew her in college. We both settled back here near Springfield."

"Does mom know her?"

He made a funny expression. Er, maybe funny wasn't the right word. He scrunched up his face with a weird, flustered sort of panic.

9

"Yes. Yes, she has met her."

I wasn't sure how to follow up, so I didn't push further. Mom was always tough on Dad's friends, so maybe there was some tension there for some reason. The timer went off—saved by the bell.

The manicotti was excellent, and we actually sat and talked for a few hours. Dad told me a bunch of old college adventure stories, but oddly enough, he didn't mention Miral again.

3

I woke up to the smell of pancakes. I quickly got ready and threw on a t-shirt and sweatpants, then headed downstairs. Walking into the kitchen, I stopped dead. There was a woman, definitely not my mom, standing *very* close to my dad.

"Tamzin... this is Miral Nefertari."

I stood there, mouth hanging open, for what seemed like an eternity.

"Hello, Tamzin. I am very pleased to meet you."

I was still stunned—I couldn't speak. This woman looked like she had just stepped out of a model fashion shoot. Her hair was raven black and she had perfectly shaped eyebrows. Her nose was thin, ending with a slight upturn. Her smile could get her out of any speeding ticket. Golden sunlight seemed to radiate from her skin. Her eyes, though... Her eyes were striking. Bright, almond-shaped orbs accentuated with an Egyptian eyeliner style.

I looked down at my t-shirt and sweats and almost felt naked. She had on a form fitting black dress with a golden belt that had an Eye of Horus as its buckle. I looked to my dad and he had on his pajama bottoms, a white t-shirt, and an old robe. He was dressed as casually as I was, but he didn't seem embarrassed at all.

"Uhm... Hi. Hi, Miral." I gave a half wave but otherwise stood entirely still.

"Please, dear, come over here." She waved me closer, and I again noticed how close she was standing to my dad. I got the feeling something went on between them, in another life.

I walked over and her perfume gently hit my nose. She even smelled great. My mom didn't wear perfume, so I wasn't really used to the smell, but Miral's was as perfect as she looked.

"Let me get a look at you," she said, gently holding my shoulders. "I haven't seen you in years. You have turned into a lovely young woman."

She had such a genuine smile that I instinctively felt safe around her. Upon close inspection, I realized that her skin was flawless—she didn't even have any wrinkles. I would have guessed that she was twenty-nine at the most, but I knew she went to school with Dad...

"Doesn't Miral look great? She hasn't aged a bit since school. You'd never guess she's around my age, would you?"

"Uhm..." I looked at the both of them, my mind still confused by her agelessness. "No. I wouldn't put her over thirty."

"Tamzin, do you remember when I babysat you when you were a little one?"

"Uhm, no. But maybe if I think about it more I'll remember." I had no recollection of her, but I was trying to see if anything about her seemed familiar.

We sat down to eat as Dad served up some pancakes. I was expecting Miral to take one or two bites, but she kept up with Dad. They both had one more pancake than I did.

"Miral always had a great appetite. She was the only girl in school that could keep up with us, both in food and beer!"

Miral didn't back down. "Oh, yes. I kept up with the boys at all times. I even kept up with your father in all of our classes."

"Clearly, she's a genius."

It was weird hearing about their past and how close they were. It probably should have bothered me more, but I realized that my dad seemed happy. With all the stress we'd been under, his happiness made me feel a little better. I didn't totally understand their dynamic, but it was okay I guess. Here was a woman that he hadn't seen much of since college—three decades or so ago—and they seemed perfectly at ease and in sync with each other, like they were picking up right where they left off.

~

I walked down the hallway, passing a group of people in white lab coats. An older man was speaking and the younger members of the group were listening while clutching pens and notepads. Two older men were walking down the hall, one holding a metal pole with an IV bag hanging from it. The second was slowly pushing a walker in front of him.

Further down the hall, there was a cluster of brightly colored shirts, all worn by people who seemed to be nurses. I turned the corner and finally found my mom's room. Walking in, I realized she already had company. It looked like they had been talking about something serious by the expressions on their faces, but they stopped as soon as they saw me come in.

"Hi, Tamzin. You remember Mayor Turner?"

The mayor turned to me and instantly put on a fake smile.

"Young Tamzin Clarke. How are you?"

"Hello, Mayor Turner."

"Please... call me Yumi."

"Hi Yumi," I replied. She stretched her hand forward and I shook it. Her grip was overly strong, but I don't think it was intentional.

"I was just telling your mother that it looks like she will be the new Chief of Police. Her excellent career and tenacity for catching crooks are paying off. There had been a few people in line before her, but..." Her eyes darted to the ground and my mom chimed in.

"With all the deaths at the hands of *Angel Jack*, we are short staffed in all areas."

The Mayor looked directly at me and said, "And, your diligence is one of the reasons *Angel Jack* was discovered and... taken out of the picture."

I wasn't sure if she knew of any of the paranormal aspects of the Ripper, so I kept my mouth shut.

"You are a worthy young woman. One with strength and fortitude." She cocked her head and seemed to be lost in thought for a moment, then continued. "Would you be willing to help me with my campaign."

"Your campaign?" I asked.

"Yes. I am running for Governor."

"Wow, that's a big step."

"Yes, yes it is… Take your time and think about it. We could use all the help we can with the campaign. You have proven yourself and would be welcome on our team."

I nodded. "Sure… I will."

"Okay, I will leave you two alone. Irene, I'm ordering you to get out of here and get back to work. We need you."

At first, I thought she was joking, but then I realized she might be serious.

"I will, Mayor. Thank you for coming by and offering me the position."

"You're welcome… And, nice seeing you again, Tamzin."

"You, too, Mayor Turner."

As she was heading out, she turned, pointed at me and said, "Yumi." Then she disappeared down the hall.

"Wow, Mom, that's cool. You will be the Chief of Police!"

"Definitely a step up, and more money, but it was such a cost." My mom's head fell to her chest. I came closer and hugged her. Trying to lighten the mood, I mentioned the Egyptian artifacts.

"We got that shipment of stuff from the pyramid in Egypt yesterday. It was pretty cool."

"Oh, really? I'll bet your dad was happy."

"Yeah. He loves that stuff."

"Did it get moved to the exhibit yet?"

"I think so. Someone came by to pick it up this morning." I wasn't sure if I should mention Miral, so I decided to be vague.

"Oh… Was it one of the students from the museum?"

"Uhh… No."

"Was it one of the curators?"

"Uhm… Yes."

"Which one? Do I know them? I'll probably have to come up to speed if I'm to be the new Police Chief."

"I think so. Dad knew her. I think her name was Miral?"

My mom's shoulders stiffened, and she squinted her eyes.

"Miral from college?"

"Yes."

"Well... I hope her skin is saggy and she's put on weight... Has she?"

"Uhm..."

She rolled her eyes, sighing. "Dammit!"

Her muscles tensed and she clenched her fists so hard that her knuckles turned white. Thank God she was on some pretty hefty pain killing meds.

"She used to date your father. I have no idea why she had such a crush on him. He only liked her because she was pretty."

The thought that came to mind was that describing her as pretty was like calling a supermodel "okay". I could definitely sense some jealousy there.

"She did say that she babysat me when I was little."

My mom squinted her eyes further and almost seemed to stop breathing... Okay, how do I get out of this? Maybe back to the Mayor?

"Wasn't Mayor Turner the Police Chief many years ago?" I already knew the answer, but if I didn't change the subject somehow Mom was going to have a stroke, strong meds or not.

"Yes, yes she was."

She seemed slightly more relaxed now. I let out a sigh of relief and felt my body loosen up. I hadn't even realized I was so tense.

"She was one of the toughest chiefs we'd had. I didn't always agree with how harsh she was."

I almost laughed. My mom was one of the staunchest women I had ever known.

"Seriously, she makes me look like a candy striper."

My eyes widened and I bit my bottom lip.

"Wow... That's pretty bad."

"Hey, I'm not that bad, am I?" She looked at me, then said, "Okay. Don't answer that."

I sat down next to my mom's bed and we watched some hospital TV. Contestants were trying to answer some questions in a limited amount of time, and the host almost always made bad jokes about them and their answers. It wasn't very amusing, but I liked being there for my mom.

After about ten minutes, I picked up the distinct aroma of fried Chinese food. There was a knock on the door and in walked Joe Berkowski holding a paper bag with some heaven inside.

"Hey, Irene. Hey, Tamzin. I couldn't break your mom out yet, so I brought her some Chinese."

"Thanks, Joe. It smells divine."

"Yeah, they try to kill you with the hospital food to keep you here longer. Thank God I broke out last week."

"You were the lucky one, Joe."

Both my mom and Joe laughed. They hugged, and I took the food. I pulled over one of the trays and wiped it down with a paper towel. Opening the bag, I pulled out the plastic plates and silverware and we all dug in.

~

It was a few hours later. Mom had drifted off to sleep, and Joe and I were watching another game show. I guess this was some kind of game show channel. He pulled his chair closer to mine.

"Hey, kiddo. Thank you for being honest with me about Daniel," he whispered. "It gave me some closure and it sounds like he went out like one of the good guys when you took down *Angel Jack*. Honestly, what are the odds that you got to meet my lost brother? I'm glad he got to meet you, even if it was for a short time..." A distant, sad look crossed his face.

"Oh my God, Joe, I completely forgot to tell you. I was down by the shore a few days ago and saw Daniel! He was able to come back."

Joe inhaled sharply, face softening. "Really? Wow... I hope I can see him."

"I can try to set something up. He was so tired from the trip back, however that works, but I bet he wants to see you."

I pulled out the dragonfly necklace to show him.

"I even got the necklace back."

"I'm still shaking my head over all of that psychic paranormal stuff, but it's good to know what happened to him."

"Well, we still don't know everything." I paused, not knowing how to tell Joe that Daniel was murdered. Here goes nothing: "I guess the reason he was able to come back was because he was murdered." It all came out of my mouth so fast...

Joe tensed, furrowing his brow. "What? What did you say?"

"He doesn't know what happened, but he does know that he was killed..."

"Fuck," he whispered under his breath. "Not Daniel. He was always such a good kid. Even though he was my older brother, he always made time for me when I needed him. I looked up to him. God... I can't believe this. I definitely need to talk to him then. We need to find out who took his life."

"Yeah, I want to help out, too."

Joe looked sadly confused, but I felt better telling him the truth about everything.

"Okay, Joe, I have to head out. Can you tell my mom I said bye?"

He still looked upset, but he sat up straighter in his seat. "Sure thing, Tamzin. I am going to stay with her until she wakes up."

"Thank you, Joe."

"Well, I mean, I don't get the game show channel at home. I need to do some binge watching." He chuckled, seemingly back to his normal self, and I laughed too, shaking my head at him.

I reached over to give him a hug, then headed out the door.

4

I was standing in a room filled with skeleton parts, chemistry equipment, glass-paned shelves, and many other bizarre items. I had no idea where I was. The moon was piercing the night sky, sending its rays through a ceiling skylight—there were no clouds to be seen.

A blinding light hit me, and I tried to cover my eyes. For some reason, my arms weren't working. I focused my eyes near the source of light and saw the ankh sitting on a long table. It lifted into the air and started moving toward a sarcophagus. It came to rest at the head of the stone container. It was standing upright, with the handle against the sarcophagus. The ankh began to spin, getting brighter and brighter with each revolution. The light was so intense that it covered my entire view...

I awoke to the sun shining through my window and sat straight up in bed. Honestly, what the hell were these visions? At least this one seemed a little more relevant because I recognized the skylight from the science museum. Weird.

I quickly got ready but was still running late. I didn't like to skip breakfast, but I had no choice today. I ran down to the kitchen to find my dad looking through the news on his new tablet.

"Hey, Dad. Gotta run, gonna be late."

"Okay, just don't make a habit of it."

I reached over to give him a kiss on the cheek.

"Dad? Did Miral take the ankh to the museum?"

"Yep. She called me last night, right before she was going to unwrap the items and give them a once over."

"Hmm... Okay," I said. I wasn't sure if the dream had anything to do with reality, but things had been pretty weird lately, so it wouldn't surprise me at this point. "I love you!"

"I love you too, Honey. Have a good day."

"I will, you too."

I raced out the door. Hopefully I'd be on time.

~

When I walked into class, the teacher was already talking at the front of the room. I saw Jimmy, Tony, and Macy sitting in their usual spots. I absolutely hated being late to class, or being late to anything in general really. When I opened the door it seemed like everyone turned to stare at me. The teacher glanced in my direction and smiled, but continued talking to the class.

I found my seat as quickly as possible, sitting in front of Jimmy, and got my things out of my bag as quietly as I could. I put my water bottle on my desk. As I was getting my notebook from my backpack, I hit the desk with my elbow, sending the water bottle crashing to the ground. It made a loud clang but luckily didn't break or spill. I cringed at the sound, giving the teacher a sheepish look. Jimmy squeezed my shoulder, chuckling at my frazzled state. Tony looked down at my water bottle, which was closest to him, then he looked up at me, shaking his head. I reached out to try and grab it off the floor, but he kicked it back towards him with his foot. He picked it up and seemed to inspect it, then tapped Macy on the shoulder, who was sitting in front of him. She turned around, raising her eyebrows at him. He held it out to her with both hands outstretched in front of him, as if he were passing her a plate of cookies. He was making faces at her, trying to convince her to take the water bottle. She gently smacked his arm, laughing quietly to herself.

"Give that back to Tam," she whispered sternly.

He let out an exaggerated sigh and turned to hold the water bottle out to me.

"For the lady who came in late and made quite the entrance," he said, bowing his head toward me.

I took the bottle from him, putting it back in my backpack so it wouldn't fall again. "Thanks for that, Tony."

"Always a pleasure."

As we were talking, the teacher announced that we were going to the computer lab to work on our projects. The class started clapping and the teacher motioned for everyone to head out. Days in the computer lab were always nice because if you weren't in the mood to do work, it was a lot easier to fool around, and if you actually wanted to be productive, you essentially had an extra hour to get stuff done.

Jimmy, Tony, Macy, and I were sitting together, which meant we weren't getting any work done. I had just opened the file for my project when Jimmy cleared his throat next to me.

"So… I didn't want to be the one to bring this up, but I'm assuming you guys are all going?" Jimmy asked quietly, looking at the screen in front of him intently like he didn't want to make eye contact.

It took the rest of us a minute to figure out what he was talking about. He meant the funeral for Paul. Just the thought of him brought back flashbacks of everything that happened. I hadn't known Paul very well, but he was still a friend.

No one said anything, we all just kind of sat there and nodded in agreement. This was something that you could never entirely get over, but we've all been trying to move on and act like things were normal again. That was really hard to do with his funeral coming up. I felt especially bad for Macy, though, because she and Paul were kind of a thing, and he died saving her—well, all of us really.

Macy looked like she was going to be sick. Tony looked from Jimmy to me, then turned to focus on Macy with the most serious expression I've ever seen from him. He put his arm around her and was stroking her hair. Even though he was trying to help, she started to cry. He jumped a little and gave me a bewildered look, but he kept his arm there.

"Hey, hey, shush. It's okay, Macy. It'll be okay, I promise," he said.

Macy nodded her head and choked out, "I know, I know. I just feel like this is all my fault."

"Macy, no. The only person at fault is Jack the Ripper, but he's gone now," I said, crossing my arms over my chest. I rested my head on Jimmy's shoulder and he let out a long sigh that seemed both frustrated and sad all at the same time.

Watching Tony and Macy together, I could definitely see them becoming more than friends. They were good for each other, balanced each other out in a way. Tony definitely seemed to have a soft spot for her. It was hard to tell with Macy, but I knew that she liked having Tony around.

I was so lost in thought that I didn't even hear the bell ring for our next class. Everyone got up and started packing up their things, rushing out of the computer lab. Macy seemed to be doing better now—she wasn't crying anymore—so that was good at least. Tony let her go so she could get up. He picked up her bag, slinging it over his shoulder.

"Oh, Tony, I can grab that," she said, motioning toward her bag.

He puffed out his chest and put his hands on his hips in a mock superhero pose. "No ma'am, I can take it from here."

Macy batted her eyelashes at him. "My hero."

"Woah, woah, woah. Lovebirds, quiet down. We can all hear you, you know," Jimmy said, getting up from his seat.

Macy rolled her eyes and started walking out. "Bye, I'll see you guys soon."

I grabbed my stuff and Jimmy and I started walking out with Tony.

"Guess I better catch up with the princess seeing as I have her stuff," Tony said, winking and leaving us alone. We followed a few moments later.

As I walked past the lockers, Jimmy pulled me aside into a little alcove in the hallway. He stood in front, holding me against the wall, and smiled wryly down at me. I was caught off guard, but I couldn't help but laugh.

"Jimmy, I can't be late again. Twice in one day is so *bad*."

"I know, I know. I'm sorry, but I couldn't help it. I feel like I've barely seen you lately."

"I'm sorry. I've just been so busy with my mom and everything else. I haven't had much free time."

"Yeah, I get that. I hope she's doing well. But I was also hoping I could take your mind off of things..." He smiled and snaked his arms

21

around my waist, pulling me closer to him. "You, me, the Puppy Palace. How about it?"

I smiled. "That sounds great, Jimmy. But, I really have to get to class now. Can't wait," I said, wriggling out of his arms. I gave him a quick kiss on the cheek, then ran to my next class, not looking back to see his reaction to my abrupt departure. I was excited to do something with Jimmy, I really was, but something felt different, off somehow. I should've been happier to be with him, but for some reason, I felt kind of weird. Whatever. It was probably just because I was out of sorts from being late to class...

~

I couldn't believe that I was here, doing this again. So many deaths in such a short period of time. Of course I didn't want to be here, no one did really, but I felt the need to come because Philip saved my life. I straightened out my skirt, took a deep breath, then walked into the viewing room where everyone was gathered. There was no body because he had been buried under the rubble, but there was still a memorial at the front of the room. Vickie's wake was pretty similar to Philip's, but Vickie's was different because she was family and everyone felt bad for me. Here there was a general sense of melancholy, which was to be expected, but people weren't going out of their way to give me their condolences. This time, it was my turn to give the condolences. I found Philip's family members, though I didn't really recognize anyone, and shook their hands.

A woman who looked like she could have been Philip's wife nodded, giving me a sad smile.

"Philip was a real hero. I wouldn't be alive right now if it weren't for him. I am eternally grateful. I'm sorry that you had to lose such a wonderful man."

"Thank you, Tamzin," she said. I was surprised that she knew my name, but I didn't question it. Maybe Philip had mentioned me. She reached out and gave me a brief hug.

All of a sudden, something, or should I say, someone, grabbed onto my leg. Before I could look down to see who it was, I heard an excited, "Tammy!"

It was Max.

"Hello, Max! I feel like I haven't seen you in forever."

Her face lit up when she saw me, but it quickly faded. She sighed and rested her head on my stomach. "Grampa Philip is gone. That makes me sad. I want him to come back."

I stroked her hair. "I know, Maxie. We all do, but it will be okay."

She looked up at me, eyes widening. "Promise?"

"Yes, promise. And do you want to hear something that will cheer you up?"

Max nodded her head up and down quickly, repeatedly saying, "Mhmm!"

"You're going to get your costumes in dance soon. But shush, don't tell anyone that I told you that."

Max started clapping, giggling about the secret that she was just told. "I want to see them now! Are they pretty?"

"You're just going to have to wait and see. But I know that you're going to like it."

She smiled at me and hugged me around the waist.

"Big sis Tamzin, will you come over to my house again? Daddy says I'm not old enough to be home alone and I wouldn't want anyone else to come and watch me."

"I would love to babysit you, Max. I can't wait to visit."

I brought Max over to a row of chairs and we sat down. Philip's actual granddaughter, Sarah, found us and started talking to Max. They were both young, but they still understood what had happened. I just hoped that I cheered Max up a little.

~

I could smell the popcorn popping. Dad and I were having a classic movie night. Ever since I could remember, I've always liked the black and white films. Tonight, we were watching *Creature from the Black Lagoon*, which was one of my favorites.

23

Dad came in with a huge bowl of popcorn—I could even smell the butter on top. My dad cooked a lot and was actually really good at it, but he specialized in pancakes and popcorn. I mean, I wasn't complaining.

"Hey, Honey. You ready for this?"

"You know it. I need some popcorn in me first, though."

"Oh, you wanted popcorn? I thought this was all for me," he said, sticking his tongue out at me. I was sitting on the couch and he stood in front of me, holding the bowl of popcorn above his head, just out of reach. I tried to grab it, but I was too short. Since Dad was stretched out to keep the popcorn away from me, I poked him in the stomach. He flinched, arms dropping to where I could reach the food. I snatched the bowl out of his hands, popping a handful of the popcorn in my mouth.

"You better save me some of that," he said, laughing and sitting down next to me on the couch.

"We'll see..."

"How has school been kiddo? Keeping up the good grades I hope."

"Yes, Dad. My grades have been pretty good. And everything at school seems to be going well."

"That's what I like to hear. I never doubted you anyway. You're my bright little girl, filled with promise."

I smiled, putting another piece of popcorn in my mouth.

"Of course, you know you got your brains from me," he said, winking.

I rolled my eyes. "Oh yeah, sure."

"How has little Maxine been? Hopefully she's holding up after Philip."

"I think she'll be okay. She's sad but stronger than we all give her credit for. She's a little trooper."

"And she has dance as a distraction. She may be young, but she's still old enough to understand what happened. I think having other activities to invest her time in will only help."

"And I told her they were getting their costumes soon so that definitely seemed to cheer her up a little bit."

"I'm glad you're so good with her. That's a good skill to have."

I nodded, thinking about that for a second. I guess I was pretty good with Max. I had never really thought about it as a skill, but I suppose certain people were better with kids than others.

"Were you not good with kids?" I asked, raising my eyebrows at him. "I mean, I think I turned out pretty well."

"Oh yes, I've always liked kids. Clearly, you also inherited that wonderful trait from me."

"Then what did I inherit from mom? My looks?" I asked, sticking my tongue out at him.

He scoffed, quickly reaching toward me to snatch the popcorn bowl.

"For that, you just lost popcorn privileges."

I pouted. "Aw, c'mon."

"I'll give the bowl back on one condition."

"What?"

"You get up to get the remote so we can get this movie started." He smiled, looking from the remote to me and back at the remote.

"Ugh... deal," I said, getting up to grab it.

I handed Dad the remote, sitting back down on the couch. He traded me the bowl, and we started up our black and white movie night.

5

Darkness surrounded me. I heard a quiet whisper and headed in that direction. My eyes slowly adjusted. I was back in the science museum. A light flashed on the wall and moved quickly to the left— someone was waving a flashlight.

Two figures were moving around near the glass shelves. The sound of their whispers hit my ears, but I couldn't make out what they were saying. The light from their flashlight flailed around for a few seconds, then the movement came to a stop.

"Here. Here it is," one of them said. The voice sounded male.

The other gave a low whistle. "Wow, it looks like pure gold."

Their flashlights were trained on a black and gold figurine of Anubis. I knew that Anubis had something to do with death and, for some reason, laughter started to ring in the back of my mind...

One of the men pulled out a glass cutter. "Are you sure there are no alarms rigged to the glass?"

"Nah, not in here. These things is not in the museum gen pop."
He chuckled.

"Wha? What you mean?"

"Never mind. Just cut. This place gives me the creeps."

The glass cutter suctioned onto the glass and the cutting blade circled around until the glass popped off.

"Got it. Grab the statue and let's go."

A hand reached into the case, and as soon as it touched the statue, I sprang into motion. Moving forward, I grabbed an arm. Yanking hard, I pulled it out of its socket. The man's scream pierced the silence.

Grasping onto his other arm, I snapped the humerus in half. He crumpled to the floor in pain, and I stomped on his femur. I could feel it snap, and some bone protruded through his pants, blood spurting out.

The other man had pulled out Anubis and started to run when he saw his partner. I moved toward him, but at a much slower pace. My hand reached out toward him, and I could feel some kind of energy radiate. This energy blasted him and he stopped dead in his tracks.

I caught up to him and circled my hand around his throat. Lifting him off the ground, he finally dropped the statue. Both of his hands latched onto mine, trying to break my hold.

Energy flowed from my arm into the thief. Blood came out of his mouth as he tried to breathe. His face became a mass of blood vessels—veins were bursting underneath his skin. Red liquid and grey matter started coming out of his ears. More and more veins popped until his eyes exploded.

I jumped up, trying to wipe the blood from my body. After a few moments, I realized that I was in my bed. Woah, that was such a vivid dream... I was so disturbed that I lay there for the next few hours, only getting out of bed when the sun started coming up.

~

I could hear the little yips before I could see them.

"I can't believe you actually brought me here," I said looking back at Jimmy, grabbing his hand and pulling him so we could get to the back of the store faster.

"I mean, who doesn't love puppies?" he asked, walking faster to pass me. As he was walking by, he snaked his arm around my waist to pull me closer to him.

"Very true."

"I can see them!" Jimmy's face lit up. I couldn't tell if this was more for me or for him, but either way, I loved seeing him happy and obviously I wasn't complaining about visiting the puppies.

When we got to the back, there was a room with a ton of cages, each puppy in their own. We could only look at them from behind a wall of glass, but if we wanted to play with one there were separate rooms to bring them to. Each cage had a tag that said the puppy's name, breed, sex, age, and cost. There were so many to look at and choose from, it was kind of overwhelming.

27

All of the puppies had their own little personalities. Even though I knew that they were happy by their wagging tails, their eyes looked so sad, like they wanted me to take them home.

"I want them all..." I said, getting as close to the glass as possible.

"Not sure how happy your parents would be if you brought one home, let alone all of them."

"A girl can dream."

"Let's take one out to play with. That's close to bringing it home, kind of. Which one do you want?"

I looked at each puppy, unsure of which to choose. I would have been okay with any of them, but one tiny puppy in the corner caught my eye. I walked closer to his cage and read the tag.

Name: Tyson, Breed: Italian Greyhound, Sex: Male, Age: 10 months, Cost: $500. He was a tiny gray and white puppy with legs that almost looked too long for his body. When I walked over, he stood up from a resting position in the cage, wagging his tail.

"Jimmy, let's look at this one," I said, pointing to the puppy, who was now panting with his tongue sticking out the side of his mouth.

Jimmy walked over to a store worker and asked if we could look at Tyson. The employee walked back into the room where the cages were, and I saw her take the pup out of the cage. She carried him to one of the playrooms, and we followed. He was wriggling in her arms, excited to get out of the cage and play.

The worker put Tyson gently on the ground, then looked back and forth between me and Jimmy.

"Have fun, and be careful with him," she said, ducking out of the room and closing the door behind her.

Jimmy and I sat on the floor facing each other, with Tyson in the middle so he could roam around and visit both of us. He walked over to Jimmy first, smelling his fingers. He began licking them, then bit playfully at Jimmy's thumb, like he was still teething.

Jimmy started patting his head, cooing, "Hey there little guy."

Tyson wagged his tail in response, rubbing his head against Jimmy's leg.

"Wow, he really likes you," I said, anxiously waiting for Tyson to walk over to me so I could pet him.

"Wouldn't it be awesome to get a dog like him some day, you know, when we're older and living together?" Jimmy asked, not taking his eyes off of little Tyson.

I froze, letting out a low, choked cough. I was happy not to have his gaze on me. Jimmy just talked about the future—*our* future. As a couple. Meaning we'd be together forever. Sure, I loved him and we've been together for so long that everything seemed to come naturally, but I couldn't think that far ahead right now. I didn't know what I wanted, not really.

Jimmy would be a nice husband, but did I want just *nice*? Did I want to be with the only guy I've ever dated for the rest of my life? If you'd asked me that question three months ago, I probably would've said yes. But now... Things were changing. *I* had changed. Everything was much more complicated, to say the least.

I think Tyson sensed my alarm because he happily padded over to me, rubbing his cool, wet nose across my leg. He nudged his head underneath my hand, and I began to pet him. I picked him up and put the pup on my lap. He rested his head on my knee and looked up, eyes almost saying, "Don't worry Tamzin. Everything will work out."

How I got that impression from a puppy, I could not tell you, but either way, it made me feel a little better.

If Jimmy realized I just had a major freak out, he didn't let on. He smiled at me, watching as I was playing with Tyson. When I found my voice again, I said, "Thank you for bringing me here. This is exactly what I needed."

"Me too, Tam. Me too."

Jimmy got off the floor and walked over to me, bending down to give me a kiss on the forehead. I closed my eyes, letting his lips brush against my skin. Behind my eyelids, I pictured a boy with blonde, spiky hair who smelled just slightly of vanilla kissing me, not the boy who was actually in the room with me. A slow ache spread through my chest. I knew that I had a hard decision to make and had to do it soon. I certainly wasn't being fair to Jimmy, seeing as I

29

wasn't giving this relationship my all. Part of my heart was elsewhere, and I didn't know how to fix it and make things go back to normal. Normal wasn't in my vocabulary anymore.

Jimmy pulled away from me, looking a little wistful for a moment. Maybe he could feel it, too. He outstretched his hand to help me get up. I took it, feeling no spark of energy from his touch. I didn't want to leave Tyson, but I knew that it was time to go. I bent down to pick the puppy up and brought him back to the woman who took him out for us.

"I hope you enjoyed your visit," she said, smiling as she cradled Tyson like a baby in her arms.

"Yes, I loved him," I said, grabbing Jimmy's hand and heading toward the door.

"Most do." Her voice rose in pitch when she said, "Don't they, Tyson? Don't they love you?"

I smiled, stealing a glance at Jimmy. He had been relatively quiet after I didn't respond to his remark about our future. I think that the reality of everything that had happened, and how we've been changed because of it, was finally weighing on the both of us...

~

The campaign office was the first floor of one of the business buildings in Springfield. It was only two blocks down from the sunken hole that used to be the Puritan Theatre. My stomach clenched as I walked by the area, but it had been surrounded by a wooden wall as the workers cleaned things up.

I think the office had formerly been a business that ultimately failed—I could see the boards that had covered the windows lying against a wall in the alley.

I was nervous, but this opportunity might help me or my family in the future. Mayor Turner had promoted my mom, so who knows what else she might be able to do. I opened the door and walked in.

Staffers, mainly other teenagers, were busy setting up tables and working on flyers. I poked my head into the back office, hoping to find our potential governor.

"Tamzin. Come on in," the mayor said as she waved me in.

"Hi."

There were a few other workers with her, most seemed to be around my age. I didn't recognize anyone from school and realized that they probably went to school in Springfield or surrounding cities. They looked up as I came in and started clapping. I stopped dead in my tracks, not sure what was happening.

"Oh, Tamzin. I told them how you helped to stop the murders. They are all very impressed that you're volunteering for me."

"Ah, okay." I awkwardly stretched out my hand to greet my now fellow co-workers.

"Hello, my name is Robert," said an extremely tall boy in a white button down shirt. He had dark hair and striking green eyes, and his voice was deeper than I expected. Definitely not a bad looking guy. He seemed nice.

"Hi, my name is Theresa, but you can call me Terry," said the very perky and very blonde girl standing close to Robert. She seemed like the type who was good at everything and always got her way. I don't know why, but something seemed off about her, fake somehow—I instantly did *not* like her. I bet she had a thing for Robert.

"John Miller. Pleased to meet you," said the last of the teens in the room. John wasn't as attractive as Robert, but he was still sort of cute in a teddy bear kind of way. He was husky and only a few inches taller than me, but he seemed like a good guy. Maybe I'd make some new friends here.

"Okay, now that introductions have been made, let's get down to our first order of business."

We all sat down. Theresa, er Terry, pulled out a pen and notepad.

"I've already had the press conference announcing my candidacy. Tamzin helped us by taking care of *Angel Jack*, so the timing was good. Stopping a serial killer gets lots of press, even if I wasn't personally responsible."

The group looked at me again. I felt pretty uncomfortable but tried not to show it.

"The first thing we need to organize is grass roots in our local communities. Each of you is from a different town. I would like you to begin by putting up flyers. Please, though, always follow your local ordinances about such things. I've had Terry work up a list of each town's requirements."

Terry handed everyone a list of dos and don'ts.

"We are going to have flyers printed up and delivered to your homes. Grab your friends and have fun with it. Hit up as much of the town as you can muster. Be safe and work in groups as much as you can. Coming off the recent killings, we all need to be extra careful."

We all nodded in agreement.

"Okay, that's pretty much it for today on my end. Please introduce yourselves to the other volunteers in the main office. We can win this!"

We all clapped, then stood up and started to head out.

"Tamzin," Yumi said, holding onto my shoulder. "How is your mom? Will she be back in action soon?"

"Dad said she should be home next week. The doctors are being extra careful about infection, and they don't want her to push it with physical activity that may cause internal bleeding."

"Okay. Please give her my best." I turned to leave as she said, "And thank you for helping out with my campaign. I need strong women on my side."

"You're welcome, Yumi. I am happy to be here." I smiled at her then turned to head out.

~

When I got home, the house was empty. It was a few hours after dinner and Dad had stayed with Mom at the hospital. I thought about how she was probably grilling him about Miral and I couldn't help but laugh. It's too weird to think about your parents' lives before you came into the picture.

I made a quick peanut butter and jelly sandwich and brought it up to my room with some milk. I sat on my bed, trying to clear my mind and just relax for once. I was finishing off my sandwich when I heard a voice.

"I am Beans!"

I jumped, almost spilling my milk, and looked over at the cymbal monkey. He didn't move or appear to look at me, but that was definitely him talking.

"Hello, Beans... You've been quiet since I brought you home."

"You rescued me. I am Beans!"

"You're welcome. And, yes, you are Beans." I smiled at him. I couldn't tell if he was cute or creepy, but I didn't get any negative vibes from him. The way he talked was pretty cute.

"Beans is worried. Beans does not like woman."

"What woman?"

I felt weird talking to him. He was a toy, and if anyone saw me having a conversation with him, they would probably think that I'd gone completely mental.

"Beans sees woman. Woman is bad."

"Can you tell me what color her hair is? Have you seen her in person?"

"She is scary woman. She hurt people."

He sounded worried so I went over to pick him up. I sat down on the bed, placing him in front of me so we could look at each other face to face. God, this was so weird.

"Okay, Beans. Talk to me. Don't make me feel more insane than I already feel right now."

"I am Beans!"

"Yes, I know," I said, letting out a long sigh. I wasn't getting anywhere with him. "Did the woman have hair like mine?"

"No. She is dark. But when she kills everyone it is gone."

"Gone? Her hair?"

"I am Beans!"

I could have been frustrated with him, but his voice seemed so childlike, so I did my best to hold my temper. I wondered if Daniel might be able to understand him or figure him out. I grabbed onto my dragonfly necklace and thought of him.

"Beans have trouble saying things. You saved Beans, and now Beans want to save you."

Suddenly a moonlit shadow crossed my fire escape. A vanilla scent wafted in on the breeze. I only knew one person who smelled like that... I heard a quiet knock, then Daniel popped his head through my curtain and stepped inside.

"Hey, you," Daniel said, cocking his head to the side and smiling. "You rang?" He pointed to my dragonfly necklace and chuckled.

"Hey," I said, unconsciously tucking a piece of hair behind my ear. "Thanks for coming."

"I will always be here if you need me."

Daniel walked over to the bed and sat down next to me. Beans slid a little bit on the blanket from the added weight. Daniel didn't even notice the cymbal monkey sitting on the bed.

"Beans sorry! Beans sorry!"

"What?" I asked.

Daniel's eyes widened and he looked at me, brow furrowed with concern. "Who are you talking to? Are you calling to other spirits?"

"No, I was just talking to Beans."

"The cymbal monkey?"

"Yeah. Did you hear him?"

"Nope, nothing."

"It's so weird. I think he's just in my head."

"They're coming to get you, Barbara," Daniel said. He put his hands out in front of him and reached for me, tongue hanging limp outside his mouth while he was making a funny face.

"What?"

"You've never heard that before? Wow, I really need to bring you up to speed on your old movies."

"Oh. Hold on. *Night of the Living Dead*, right?"

"Yep."

"I wasn't really paying attention. I'm worried about what Beans has to say. He's such a fickle little guy."

"Is he talking now?"

"No. He said he was sorry, then stopped."

"What a life you live, Tamzin Clarke... I hope you know that normal is overrated anyway."

I laughed and snuggled up closer to him. I put my head on his shoulder and ran my fingers up and down his arm. He felt so warm, so tangible, so *alive*. I didn't understand why I was drawn to him, but he made me feel relaxed, like I could be myself with him no matter what. He gave me a sort of validation that I didn't get from anyone else.

I felt guilty about liking Daniel, but part of me tried to rationalize my feelings to make some of the guilt go away—he was a ghost, so clearly it didn't even count. I knew that was B.S. because no matter what he was my feelings were still there, but I didn't know what that meant for our future. Or if we could even have one. I knew that he liked me, but was it unfair to be with him now knowing that we couldn't really be together? I wasn't sure if I was just making things worse for the both of us or not.

We laid together for a while. Daniel held my hand tightly and we relaxed, enjoying the closeness. A million things were going through my head right now, but one thing in particular seemed to keep coming up, and I couldn't avoid talking about it any longer.

I cleared my throat, shifting my body to face Daniel. "Your brother wants to see you. Is that okay?" I asked quietly, not knowing how he'd react.

Daniel paused, contemplating. "He was younger than me back then and now he's old." He said it so matter of fact and devoid of emotion. I thought he was going to say something else, but the silence in the room grew.

"Well, he's still your brother."

"I know, but things aren't the same."

"That's okay, though. Just because things are different now doesn't mean you shouldn't see him. It's been so long, Daniel. He never even knew what happened to you. I can't imagine what it would be like to lose a sibling, especially at such a young age."

"You don't have siblings to lose."

I sighed, rolling my eyes. He was being difficult on purpose. "I know, I know. I'm just saying."

"But that's just it. It has been so long, too long. I don't know if I can face him. Not legitimately. I know I've already seen him, but we never got to talk. This... this is just so much more terrifying."

"You think that talking with Joe is more terrifying than fighting Jack the Ripper?"

Daniel clenched and unclenched his fists, not looking at me. "I don't know."

"I think you should see him."

"I'm scared, Tam," he said, so quietly that I almost didn't hear him. His voice sounded sort of gravelly, like he was going to start crying. "He's moved on. He's got a new life now. One that I'm not a part of."

"That doesn't mean he's completely forgotten about you, Daniel. Now that you're here, you can make yourself part of his life again."

"But what happens when I'm gone for real? I can't let him lose me twice."

I hadn't really thought about that before. I suppose it would be hard for Joe to finally have his brother back, only to lose him again. I thought about Vickie and how happy I was to see her one last time, even though I knew she couldn't stay. "Trust me, it'll be harder on him if he doesn't see you. I think you both need some closure and this is the only way you're going to get it."

Daniel went silent for a long time—my words hung in the air. I didn't want to press him further, but I hoped he would see Joe. They both deserved to find happiness, even if it was for a short period of time.

"Okay," he said.

"Okay, what? Okay, you're going to see him or okay, stop talking right now Tamzin?"

Daniel chuckled, shaking his head at me. "Yeah, I should see him."

I hugged him, and he put his arm around my shoulders, allowing my head to rest on his chest.

Daniel cleared his throat, and I could feel his breaths quicken. "I meant it when I said I was falling in love with you... I know that things are complicated, but I hope you keep me around. Regardless of how you feel, I want to be there whenever you need me."

I had no idea what to say because I honestly wasn't sure how I felt. I didn't know if this was love or something else, but I guess it didn't really matter right now. I squeezed his hand tightly in response.

My eyes were getting heavy, and I knew that I was about to fall asleep. The last thing I heard before everything went dark was:

"Beans sleepy, too." Then there was a quiet yawn.

6

I was standing in the courtyard, surrounded by thousands of people. Once again, I noticed the sculptures and massive pillars against the walls. I was on a dais with about twenty other people. The prince was there, standing beside the high priestess. The pharaoh himself presided over the ceremony—his robes were the most lavish. His headdress also had the scarab symbol on it. I could see the pride and love in Amenhotep's eyes for his son.

Looking out into the courtyard, there was a long set of stairs leading up to our platform. I could see the balcony we had stood on before, which housed the bed chambers. There was a line of well-dressed dignitaries on either side of the stairs. The road leading to the stairs was lined with soldiers three deep. Behind them were the throngs of people. I got a general feeling of happiness from everyone. Most of the people looked well fed, even the elderly.

I was standing on the side of the dais with the prince. There seemed to be a few other relatives, as well as other servants, standing here with me. One person stood out in particular—a boy who looked just like the prince. My best guess would be that he was his younger brother and that they were only about two years apart.

On the other side of the platform was the high priestess and her followers. They all had ankh symbols on their robes and the bride-to-be was holding the ankh scepter. Even in the stark sun during the day, the ankh gave off light that made it hard to look at.

"My son, Amenhotep the second, shall become one with our high priestess, Hatshepsut. They will become a single entity, beginning their journey in life and blazing defiantly into the afterlife. They will make many children and give back to our people tenfold. Their bond will be sacred. None shall tear them asunder."

I felt both angry and scared. Hatshepsut was using the prince as a stepping stone. She did not seem to have any love for Amenhotep II. I was forbidden to speak about such things, but I was torn because I loved my master. He was kind and benevolent. We used to talk frequently before the priestess got close to him. I wanted to believe that he had some passion for me, but I wasn't sure if he was marrying her because he had to or because they had some kind of bond.

As the ceremony concluded, I began to cry. I could not protect the man that I loved.

I gently regained consciousness, noticing that Daniel had left. The first rays of sunshine were coming up. My dream made me feel sad, almost like a part of me had been taken away somehow. It felt like I had just been crying, even though I knew I hadn't. It was only a dream, but I wondered if it could have been true… I noticed that Beans was still on the bed. What did he mean when he was talking about the "bad woman"?

~

The funeral for Paul couldn't have been more fitting. It would have been what he wanted if he could have been here to see it. It was perfectly spectacular yet not too over the top. Paul always did say he wanted to go out with a bang… And he was always one to enjoy attention. The church was decorated with extra flower arrangements and there were a ton of people here. The ceremony itself was beautiful. They played some of Paul's favorite songs and even put on original music the band had made. The people who spoke on Paul's behalf brought the crowd to tears. Jimmy, Tony, Macy and I were sitting in a pew in the second row, getting ready to rise and leave the church.

I wasn't extremely close to Paul, but his loss still hit me hard. Just the thought of never seeing him again, never hearing his voice again, was incomprehensible. I knew exactly how his family felt, and my heart went out to them. To lose a son, no matter what age he was, is tragic. Sitting through the funeral was painful, and it only reminded me of Vickie's. We've had to endure far too much loss lately, and I think we were all ready for something to finally go right.

I looked over at my friends, and we all shared a similarly pained grimace. Tony and Macy got out of the pew first, and I saw Macy grab for Tony's hand as they walked down the aisle. He enclosed her hand in his and gave it a squeeze. Jimmy and I followed close behind.

When we got out to the front of the church, I took a deep breath—I hadn't even realized I'd been holding it. The cool breeze felt good on my face.

"Well friends, we've made it this far…" Tony said, shifting just a tiny bit closer to Macy.

"I guess so," Macy said quietly, shaking her head. "We shouldn't even have to be here right now. All of this is so unfair."

"I know, it really is," Tony said, knitting his eyebrows.

"Who's gonna sing for the band now?" Macy asked, sounding slightly alarmed. "We can't go on without Paul! No one else can even sing. Jimmy, what are you going to do?"

"I don't know," Jimmy said, rubbing his temples with his fingers, almost as if he could erase the fact that Paul was gone.

"I guess we'll just have to find another singer… Maybe hold a tryout?" I said, rubbing my hand on Jimmy's back to try to comfort him.

"That sounds like a rockin' idea, Tam," Tony said, nodding his head in approval.

"Yeah, we'll figure it out. I can't really think about that much right now. The band will manage," Jimmy said.

We nodded slowly, standing together in silence outside the church. No one knew what to do or say, we were all out of words at this point. I gently pushed Jimmy closer to Tony and Macy and put my arms around everyone as best I could. We all needed a hug, so I figured a group hug would be nice. Everyone reciprocated, lifting their arms and encircling their neighbor. We stayed like that, hugging outside the church, taking comfort in each other's closeness and not saying a word, until everyone else had left.

~

Going to dance class could solve just about any problem, for the short period of time I was in the studio that is. Dance could take my mind off of things like nothing else could. Macy seemed to be feeling the same way because she looked a little perkier than she had been recently.

When I walked into the studio, Macy looked genuinely happy to see me. She patted the area on the floor next to her, motioning for me to sit with her, even though these were our usual stretching spots. I smiled, plopping down next to her.

"I can't believe we're getting so close to finishing our routine!" she said, tapping the floor in front of her to the beat of our dance song.

"I know. It's gone by so quickly."

"Maybe we'll finish it up today."

"That would be awesome if we did." I paused, wondering if I should ask what I wanted to ask. I decided to go for it. "So, you and Tony?" I wiggled my eyebrows at her.

She whipped her head around at the mention of his name, scrunching her nose. "Oh, him? I don't know."

"But you guys are totally into each other. It's pretty obvious."

She scoffed. "Oh my God, it is NOT obvious."

"So you do like Tony!"

She raised her hands in the air toward me, trying to shush me. "Quiet, Tamzin! Not so loud."

"It's not like he can hear me, Macy. It's just you and me. I'm sure no one else cares about your love life. Besides, they don't even know Tony."

She looked around the room, a panicked expression crossing her face. "You don't know that."

"Even if they did, it would be fine. If anything, he'd love to hear that you liked him."

"I honestly don't know how I feel right now, okay? Can we not talk about this?"

"Oh, sure. You 'don't know how you feel'," I said, making air quotes. "Fine. Does that mean we can talk about this another time?" I looked at her sidelong, shining my brightest smile her way.

41

She rolled her eyes, laughing.

Right on cue, our instructor finally started the music and we went through the usual routine. We stretched, did some across the floor warm-ups, then practiced our dance for the recital. We were getting close to finishing the routine, but still had a lot to work on. Things were coming along well, though, so I didn't have much to complain about. Sometimes it's better to learn the moves in smaller segments, giving us more time to master the flow before learning too much. Half the time people forget the new stuff we learn anyway.

On the way out, I stopped to give Macy a hug. I don't know why I did it because we didn't normally hug when we said goodbye to each other, but it just seemed like the right thing to do. She didn't act surprised. Instead, she held onto me tightly, like she really needed this hug, then squeezed.

"He likes you!" I sang after pulling away.

Walking outside I heard a faint, "Shut up!" through the closing door.

7

I was waiting on the shore of the river where I had first met Daniel. Dragonflies buzzed around as a soft breeze ruffled my hair. Joe Berkowski was coming to see his brother—this would be the first time they had truly met since Joe lost Daniel, aside from when we were fighting for our lives. Daniel brought me some closure with Vickie, so I hoped I could do the same for Joe and help him come to terms with Daniel's disappearance. He was only eight years old when his brother disappeared.

I sat down and let the warm breeze brush across my face. A green dragonfly buzzed around me and came to rest on my hand. Another one zipped around my head, landing directly on top. Another one landed on my leg. They seemed to be attracted to me or something.

"Ahem." I heard from behind me.

"Hey, Daniel." I tried to talk without moving so I wouldn't scare the dragonflies away, but I still ended up making the bug on top of my head leave.

"You should have seen your face when that one landed on your head. I'm not sure I could mimic that look even if you paid me."

"Ha-ha, very funny," I said.

Daniel came over and sat beside me. The other two dragonflies took off, and now we were alone. He moved to give me a quick kiss on the cheek, but I turned my head so his lips would meet mine.

"Ahem, you two."

I jumped, cheeks reddening, and we pulled apart. I recognized the voice, though, and got up.

"Hi, Joe."

"Hey, Tamzin." He gave me a soft hug and stepped back to look at Daniel.

"I'm telling you, man, this is crazy."

Daniel looked at his now much older brother. At first, he seemed hesitant, not saying anything. Then he finally spoke up. "Joey, what happened to you?"

They both smiled and hugged tightly. Tears started to well up in Joe's eyes, but he managed to hold them back.

"Nah, Daniel. I get to ask you what happened, not the other way around. I got old, plain and simple. You disappeared."

"I really don't know, Joey. The last thing I remember was being here on this beach. Then, I was just drifting off in some ghost land. I only came back when I saw Tamzin."

"Really?"

"Yeah. I had seen some people here before, but I was drawn to Tamzin. For whatever reason, I tried to talk to her and it worked."

"So, you got nuthin' on what happened?"

"Like I told Tamzin, it's like a blank space. I have no idea."

"But… She said you were murdered?" Joe hesitated when he said "murdered", like he still didn't want to believe it. I don't think any of us wanted to.

"Yeah… I can't explain it, but I know that someone killed me. I don't know if it was malicious or accidental, but there is a certainty in my ghost gut that knows it's a fact."

"Oh… I still don't understand. I don't see how this could've happened to you. I'm sorry." Joe's voice trailed off. He seemed to be deep in thought, a mix of emotions crossing his face. It wasn't normal for Joe to be so vulnerable.

The silence was deafening. I had to say something to get both of them talking again. "I think we should try to find out what happened. What do you guys think?" I asked, already knowing their answer.

"Yep," they both said in unison, nodding. I could see the similarities in their mannerisms now, even though they didn't really look alike from what I could tell.

"When you disappeared, I went back into my shell. I was confused. Part of me blamed you, and part of me blamed me," Joe said, not meeting Daniel's eyes.

"It wasn't your fault, Joey."

"I know that now... It just took me a helluva lot of time and energy to get there."

"I'm sorry, Joey."

Joe stood up straighter, fixing his jacket. "Nah, don't be sorry. Shit happens. I've seen tons of it over my years on the force."

"Maybe we can pull up your old files from work that may pertain to Daniel?" I said.

"Yeah. Yeah, we can do that." Berkowski looked at Daniel and smiled. "And, I became a cop because of what happened to you. So maybe all of this happened for a reason?"

"Maybe, Joey. Maybe it did."

"And your mom, Tamzin. The new chief! Congrats. She is gonna bust my... Ah, yeah."

We all laughed, and Joe and Daniel gave each other another hug.

"Okay, I gotta get back. You have to come by my house sometime and meet the family. Both of ya," Joe said, looking back and forth between me and Daniel. His gaze lingered on Daniel and a mixture of confusion, pain, and happiness crossed his face.

"Absolutely... Although I'm not sure how we can introduce me," Daniel said, averting his eyes.

"Hmm... Yeah, you're right. Maybe you two can come by together. They knew Vickie pretty well, as well as Tamzin's mom. We can just introduce you as Tamzin's boyfriend."

Daniel seemed to like the thought of that. I, on the other hand, felt guilty about Jimmy. I really didn't know what to do.

Joe and Daniel said their goodbyes, and Joe headed up the trail. I lingered behind. Maybe it would be a good thing to have me and Daniel practice playing couple.

~

I was standing next to the sarcophagus. Its stone top was sitting on the floor. One of the inner coffins was opened on top of it. The face on the coffin was intricately carved with sections of gold and blue. On the head of this carving was the scarab beetle. The

45

person depicted must have been a worshipper of the beetle, like Amenhotep and his son.

I moved closer to a lit area but stopped short of revealing myself. I heard two people arguing—a man and a woman. The woman's voice was low and calm, but the man sounded very angry. He had some kind of middle eastern accent. I could only make out some of the conversation.

"You have no right to these artifacts. They belong in their home country!"

The woman's voice was much quieter. "We sponsored the dig and have every right to show the exhibit prior to bringing all the antiquities back to your home."

"Just because you throw around your money does not make you have right! These are our ancestors, not yours!"

"Without our funds, you would never have known this buried pyramid existed. We are studying and exhibiting for six months. After that time, you will have sole custody."

"It is not right!" The man stomped forward toward the woman, and shouted, "You have no right!"

He raised his fist as if he were going to hit her. She slowly backed away, and I was suddenly upon the man. I caught a glimpse of the back of the woman walking down between the shelves as if nothing was happening here.

The man looked at me with horror.

"NO! You cannot be!"

I grabbed his arm and snapped the bone.

"AHHH! Stop. Please stop!"

My hand grabbed his throat and slammed him down onto one of the chemistry tables. His arm hung lifelessly over the edge. The rest of his body flailed and tried to move, but his head was pinned.

My other arm waved over his head, and I felt a pulse of energy. His body kept thrashing around, trying to get loose, but his head didn't budge. It was then that I saw the weirdest thing—frogs...

Dozens of frogs were hopping around the table. The man looked at them with a frown, and he stopped flailing for a moment as he tried to figure out what was happening. Then, it started.

One frog jumped directly at his head. It slammed into him and bounced off. Then, other frogs started jumping. Harder and harder they came. These were definitely not normal frogs.

They started to target his mouth and eyes. At least two of them went in his mouth and he started thrashing with even more vigor. They started hitting his eyes, slamming him with great force. Finally, one of them smashed right through his eyeball. I could feel him try to scream, but the sound was muffled by the frogs in his mouth.

Harder and harder, the frogs tore at his body. His teeth shattered and his other eye exploded. They were swarming him, pummeling his cheekbones and nose. Crack, crack. I felt his face being broken. One final smash and his skull crushed inward. His dancing body finally stopped.

The frogs started hopping away, covering the table and floor. When enough had cleared away, I saw my hand. It was skeletal with bits of dried flesh. I fainted…

I woke up, my whole body shaking. What was happening to me? Did the scarab and the visions of the past have something to do with these nightmares? I grabbed Beans and put him on the table next to my bed. He made me feel a little better.

"Zzzzz…" I heard from him. Yep, he was definitely my bodyguard. Nothing would get past him.

Sleep did not come easily that night.

8

I hopped out of bed and put myself together, getting fully dressed this time just in case my dad had any visitors. Running downstairs, I was relieved to see my dad, alone, flipping the final pancake.

"Hey, Honey."

"Hi, Dad. The pancakes smell great!"

"My specialty... They never fail to get five stars."

"No Miral today?"

"No. She's been busy with the exhibit."

"How's it going?"

"Quite well, actually. She did hit a snag with the Egyptian embassy, though. Apparently, there were some protests about the pieces from the tomb leaving Egypt."

"Really?" I immediately thought of my dream.

"Yeah. She's been waiting on the canopic jars."

"Aren't those the containers for a mummy's organs?"

"Yep. She's been excited about their arrival, but of course has been hit with this political wrangling. She was expecting a visit from some dignitary yesterday. Miral was hoping he would support her side, but she wasn't sure."

"It's weird—I had a dream about something like that last night. Some guy was hassling the museum. He ended up getting beaten to death by frogs."

My dad chuckled. "That sounds more like a nightmare to me, Tam."

"Yeah, I guess it was. My dreams have been up and down... and very Egyptian lately."

"Must be the exhibit getting into your subconscious."

"I guess..." Or a scarab getting under my skin?

We sat down and started eating.

"Dad? The scarab brooch in the back room in the store… Where'd you get it from?"

"Scarab? Oh, yes… That one had your name on the shipping manifest… I thought it was just a mistake, but I couldn't find anything in my records about it."

"My name? That's weird."

"It is quite beautiful, isn't it?"

"Yeah, I love it," I said, almost involuntarily.

"Well then, it's yours. First that dragonfly necklace and now the scarab brooch. You are becoming a real bug collector." He said that with the usual Dad laugh. He always amused himself with his own jokes.

"Ha-ha, funny." I stuck my tongue out at him.

In between bites of the pancakes, he said, "I'm going to see your mom today. She's getting antsy. She wants to get sprung from the hospital."

"I hope she stays until the doctors give her the okay. She's so stubborn sometimes."

"Yep, she's the most stubborn woman I know," he said, looking off into space as if his mind was elsewhere.

We were finishing up our pancakes when I remembered I had to tell him about what I was doing after school.

"Oh, Dad, I'm going to be with Jimmy after school today. Helping out his band."

"Okay. How are they doing? I mean, since Paul…?"

"They're doing the best they can. I think the fact that he died fighting against the Ripper kind of helped all of us. We're looking for a new singer today. Not sure how it will go…"

"Well, please give Jimmy my regards. I hope they find someone."

"I will."

I got up and gave him a kiss on the cheek.

"Love you, Dad."

"I love you, too, Honey."

~

I was standing outside the Rivoli Theater. It had been a regular movie theater many years ago. Now, it was a small venue created from the front lobby and offices. Jimmy played more intimate performances here, but today the whole group came along for the audition. Tony knew the owners, which helped out money-wise. We got to use the place for free today.

"Hey, Babe, come on in," said Jimmy, all smiles.

"Just one sec. I'm waiting for Macy while you guys finish setting up."

"Okay," he said, pulling me in for a quick kiss.

"Dudes! The party chairman and his fine chairess are here!" Tony said, walking hand in hand with Macy. She was grinning and seemed pleased with herself.

"Hey, guys," I said.

"Dude," said Jimmy, holding his hand up in the air.

"Dude..." Tony raised his hand up and they both came down in a hearty shake. "Rock on!"

We entered as the rest of the group was finishing setting up. Nothing was too fancy, as this was more of a practice session than a real gig. They had advertised at school, with free ads online, and had even taken out an ad in the paper. There were about fifty chairs, and maybe ten potential singers along with their entourages. They were mostly young teenagers, but there was also one man who had wrinkles and a scraggly beard. Most were guys, but there were two girls in the lineup that looked like they were going to kill it.

Tony grabbed a mic and stood front and center. "Okay, folks. We are here looking for a new lead singer. To be totally up front, we lost Paul to the Ripper and his henchman. He died a hero. There are to be no tears tonight. This is a celebration of Paul, and we honor him with our jams. The music shall continue!"

Jimmy whispered to the other members of the group, and they grabbed their instruments.

"Okay," continued Tony. "We mentioned one song in the ads. We hope you came prepared. If you didn't, please let us know why.

This will be a strike against you, but if you have a good excuse and have the skills, you can still make the cut."

Macy had been going to the would-be singers with a signup sheet. The last potential member signed it and she handed it to Tony.

"Okay," he said, squinting at the paper. "The first victim looks like... Boob?"

Macy cringed and rolled her eyes, grabbing the paper.

"Tony! It's Boone."

"Oops... My bad."

The wrinkly fellow stepped out of his row of seats and came up to the mic. Everyone kind of stared at him, since he was at least twice the age of everyone else in the band.

"Okay, folks. Let's welcome Boone to the band tryouts!"

We gave a small, but full round of applause. Boone grabbed the mic like a pro and nodded his head. The group launched into the Star Spangled Banner, and Boone sang away. He did a pretty good job, and when he stopped singing the crowd and the band gave him a nice round of applause.

"Thank you, thank you." He nodded to the audience and stepped back down to find his seat.

"Next up, we have..." Tony looked at Macy, who mouthed *Travis*. "Travis! Travis, please come on down."

The youngest looking contender came up. His hand was shaking as he took the mic. He waved to everyone and tried to smile. It was hard not to notice his braces. Regardless, the crowd clapped as they did for Boone. The boy nodded a few times and just stood there.

Jimmy quietly said to him, "No rush. Start when you're ready."

That seemed to calm Travis somewhat. He closed his eyes and nodded. Jimmy gave a four count and they started playing.

Travis got an A for effort, but a C for quality. We clapped, and Travis looked very glad to get back to his seat. His mom was with him and she nodded her approval. She was right to be proud—it took a lot of guts just to get up there.

We went through the rest of the potential singers and finally came to Vanessa. She looked like she was around our age, with black hair and a lot of piercings. She exuded confidence when she took the mic and when she started to sing, we all did a double take. Her voice was smooth and perfectly on key. She got to the last verse of the song and motioned for Jimmy's band to play louder. They played harder and she turned the song into a rock anthem.

The entire room stood up and clapped as hard as they could. Tony's eyes were wide and his mouth was open. Macy was holding his arm and even she seemed dumbfounded. Tony came to life and went back to the mic.

"Well, I think we have a winner! Vanessa, that was awesome!"

Jimmy stepped forward and shook her hand. He took the mic for some final words.

"I'd like to thank everyone for taking the time to come out this afternoon. Vanessa has given a great performance, but we still need to work out details and make sure she's a good fit. We will keep your information on file, and you may still hear from us. Once again, though, thank you for coming. Let's give a huge round of applause for all of our singers!"

We clapped for a while and then the crowd started to leave. Jimmy was talking with Vanessa, and things seemed to look good for her. She could definitely sing, that's for sure.

~

Macy and I stood at the front of the room, looking at each of the little girls sitting in front of us. Max was there, staring up at me with big, wonder-filled eyes, just like the rest of her classmates. We had just about finished their class for the day, but they all knew what was coming now—the surprise was hanging on the portable racks at the side of the room. Macy and I were waiting just a few seconds longer to give them their costumes.

Macy clapped her hands together, then said, "All right ladies... Are you ready to try on the costumes?"

The room filled with high pitched squeals and some of the girls started to clap excitedly.

"Tammy! I want to see my costume!" Max yelled, getting up from her spot on the floor, running over to me. She tugged at the bottom of my shirt, pouting up at me.

"Yes, Max. I'm going to get them right now. But I won't be able to move if you don't let go of my shirt." I stuck my tongue out at her and she quickly let me go, running back to the middle of the room with her arms crossed at her chest.

When we finally gave each of the girls their costumes and they pulled their outfit out of the bag, they were more than ready to try them on. We're supposed to have the girls try the costumes on to make sure they fit correctly, and then the class gets to do one run-through of their routine dressed up.

"Is this on right?" Max asked, rubbing her belly where the sequins of the costume were fastened.

Macy was walking around, helping the girls put their costumes on. I walked over to Max to help her.

"Max, you have it on backward!"

She started giggling and rubbing her belly more. "No, no. I like it this way better!"

I turned the leotard around, putting the costume on her correctly. When the girls were all dressed, they were looking at themselves intently in the mirror. They all looked great and seemed to be happy with our choice.

When they were done staring at their reflections, they got into position and I started their song. Macy and I sat in the front, watching as they worked through the moves. They were doing a good job staying in time with the music, which is all that really mattered right now.

When the song ended, the girls grabbed their bags but didn't want to take their costumes off.

"Be careful with them. Don't get them dirty!" Macy called as they filed out of the room.

Max ran out with her hands above her head and I could hear her say, "Daddy, Daddy! Look at me."

"You look very pretty my little Maxine."

Even though I couldn't see her, I knew she was smiling up at him, probably rubbing her belly.

9

It was dark. I was standing in the middle of rows upon rows of pillars extending so high that their tops ended in darkness. It looked like some kind of outside courtyard.

I spied the priestess walking, looking behind and around her occasionally. She had an air of nonchalance, but I knew that she was up to no good. I crept behind the pillars, moving stealthily from one to the next until we came to a garden area. The "wall" of shrubs was well over our heads, obscuring her after she entered. I knew it was risky, but I followed her into the mass of foliage and flowers.

As I entered, a great earthen scent came to me. It was mingled with what I could only describe as some kind of dense green forest. I wasn't sure where that thought came from—probably something from the mind of the slave girl.

I moved forward, trying to be as quiet as possible. Two columns of shrubs lined the path, and they seemed to open into a larger area at the end. There were roses interspersed with yellow chrysanthemums climbing the walls, their perfume getting stronger as I crept along.

I came to the opening, clinging to the edge, hoping not to be spotted by my nemesis. I peeked around the corner and spied her heading into another pathway of shrubs. After a moment, I hopped out into the garden courtyard. This area had small pools of lotus flowers, many of which had grape vines enclosing them on trellises.

I sprinted to the other pathway. This one opened out into a large poppy field with a swing in the middle. It was beautiful, but the servant girl was mortified by what she saw—the priestess was holding hands with the boy from the wedding! I knew that this was definitely the prince's younger brother.

The traitor looked around one last time to make sure there was no one watching. I ducked back quickly so she wouldn't see me, then *carefully peeked my head out to see what was going on. They were kissing! I was so angry that I thought I was going to burst.*

I woke up with both of my fists tightly clenched. Wow, these dreams were really getting to me... I had feelings and thoughts that seemed to be from a servant in the old Egypt visions. But then there were also the nightmares that revolved around the *Mummy Extravaganza*. Everything was so vivid—I could even taste the dry air and smell the musty tomb artifacts! Hopefully things would settle down when Mom came home and our family was back together.

~

"Hi, Nomi," I said, entering my mom's hospital room.

"Well hello, young Tamzin. It is good to see you." Nomi was our resident expert on magic. She did tarot and palm readings two doors down from my dad's antique store. She was known as "Madame Zortal". I didn't know if her readings were only a means to an end—you know, a way to make money—but either way, she did have a lot of knowledge of the arcane arts and all things paranormal. She helped us defeat Jack the Ripper and immediately knew that Daniel was "different".

I gave my mom a hug.

"Hey, Honey." She fidgeted and looked at the clock. As much as I wanted to, I couldn't bust her out. The doctors were adamant about keeping her here for a couple more days.

"Hi, Mom. I love you. What are they saying now about your release?"

She rolled her eyes. "Two more damn days."

"Irene, it is best you heal properly. You are now going to be tasked with running the entire police department, which includes picking up all the pieces that have fallen."

"I know, I know," Mom said. "I just keep wanting to move, move, move. Being stuck here is worse than being tortured."

"And Mom used to say that *I* had ants in *my* pants."

She laughed. "Yes, I did. You wouldn't stop moving. Your dad and I got lots of extra exercise as we followed you around, keeping an eye on you."

Nomi smiled and chimed in. "Oh yes, Tamzin. They used to have me babysit to get a respite from those little legs running every which way. They'd sneak back in, making sure they didn't wake you. Didn't want to rouse the gremlin!"

"I remember those days. We loved her to death, but she was very headstrong," Mom said, looking a little wistful.

"Okay... enough laughs at my expense." I sat down next to her bed, with Nomi on the other side. We were quiet for a few moments, but there was no awkwardness.

My mom sat up in bed, looking at her television. She fiddled with the volume control on her remote and the monotone voice of Dan Defino filled the room. Sometimes I thought he must have been a comedian before becoming the voice of our local news channel.

"This is the story we've been reporting on this week." The video went to a shot of an alley in the downtown area. There was a distinct lack of homeless, which were often lining the steam vents. "Our homeless population has gone from many to almost non-existent. Here is John Champlain, the organizer of the local soup kitchen."

"Yeah, man. Take a look." He said this with a broad sweep of his arm, revealing an empty dining area. "The other day, I noticed fewer and fewer guys. Some of the regulars disappeared. Now, today, nothin'. They all done packed up and gone somewhere."

Champlain shrugged his shoulders, opened his eyes wide, and shook his head with bewilderment. The television then switched back to Dan Defino's talking head.

"Very weird things, indeed. Maybe this had to do with people leaving because of *Angel Jack*? We will continue to report on this story."

The TV cut to a commercial.

"Very worrisome," said Nomi. "With the Ripper gone, I had hoped the energies would calm down."

"What do you mean, Nomi?" asked my mom.

"I have felt a stirring. Strong magics at work. They chill my bones, and I fear darkness once again envelops everyone."

"I'm not sure I will survive another supernatural event." My mom shook her head. "The last one nearly killed me."

I was about to say something when the news came back on.

"In other news, a missing diplomat has been reported. Abdul Sharif was on a tour that came to Springfield this past week. If you have any information, please contact the authorities."

An image of an older man popped up on the screen. My stomach fell—it was the guy from my dream! The one who had been "frogged" to a pulp.

Nomi must have noticed the expression on my face.

"Are you okay, Tamzin? Girl, you look like you just saw a ghost."

Little did she know how accurate her expression was.

"Uh, I'm not sure. I had a weird dream with that guy in it, the diplomat. He was killed."

"Well, if it was a dream, then it couldn't be true," Mom said.

Her cop gut was kicking in, and I hoped it was right. But, after all the recent insanity, I couldn't be sure.

"What happened to him in the dream, honey?"

"Frogs attacked him. They pretty much ground him into mincemeat. It was gross."

"Well, that's good. It couldn't have been real then," Mom repeated.

Nomi looked at Mom, her eyes wide and her lips taut. I could tell she wanted to say something, but she kept it to herself.

"Okay... I must be leaving you both. Please, Irene, finish healing and come back to us."

"I will. I promise."

She gave my mom a hug.

"And you, Tamzin girl, come by to see me when you can. Understood?"

I nodded my head.

"Yes, Nomi." I saluted at her order, the misgiving in her eyes telling me that she was serious. She headed out, and I sat with my mom as we joked about the rest of Dan Defino's delivery of the newscast.

~

Heading back home, I went directly to Dad's antique shop. It was Sunday, and I had organizing duty. Dad stayed for the morning while I was visiting Mom, and now he was going to make a delivery, then go to see her later.

"Dad? Are you here?" I asked as the bell chimed on the door.

"Hey, honey, I'm in the back."

Ah, the *Dungeon of Curious Oddities*. Dad was often back there for hours, detailing the incoming items and prepping them for a sale or delivery. He broke through the curtain, gingerly carrying a piece of pottery. He put it down on the counter.

I gave him a quick hug and kiss as he nodded toward the artifact.

"A canopic jar for the exhibit."

I studied it for a moment—the cap of the jar seemed to be carved into a jackal's head.

"Duamutef is the jackal-headed god. This jar contains the stomach."

"Oh, cool."

"I'm bringing it to Miral this afternoon. It was the last part of the main pharaoh excavation."

"Aren't you visiting Mom today? She was pretty antsy this morning. I think she wanted me to break her out."

"Oh, yes. I should get to your mom a bit later."

"Dad... Did you hear about the Egyptian diplomat that was visiting? Was he at the exhibit?"

"Ah... I think so. Miral said that he approved her request to open the exhibit. There was apparently some confusion with the political red tape, but it was resolved."

"Okay. I had a weird dream about the exhibit. I guess I've got mummies on my mind."

"Mummies on my mind! That's probably a better title than the *Mummy Extravaganza* for the exhibit. I should mention that to Miral."

My dad chuckled, but I still had a knot in my stomach.

"Did I mention that this jar contains a stomach?" he asked, like he knew something was up with me. There was a twinkle in his eye as he teased me.

"Gross." I stepped back from the jar, and my knot turned from a misgiving to *don't put me in there*!

"Okay, I'm heading out. Keep an eye on things, and don't forget to lock up when you close."

"I won't, Dad."

He gave me a kiss on the forehead.

"Love you."

"I love you, too, Dad"

And with that, he headed out with his prize.

~

It was a few hours later. I closed the store and was sitting on my bed when my cellphone rang.

"Tamzin?"

It was my mom.

"Hey, Mom. What's up?"

"I was expecting your dad, is he there?"

"Uh... no. He was making a delivery and said he'd drop by later."

"When was this?"

"Mid-afternoon, maybe around three?"

"I tried calling him, but he didn't answer."

"That's weird. Dad always keeps his phone close for emergencies."

"Where was his delivery?"

I thought about it for a second, but I knew that when my mom was tracking someone down, she was serious. I was hesitant, but I still told her.

"He brought the final canopic jar to the museum."

The phone was silent for a few seconds.

"You mean to Miral, don't you?"

I really didn't want to get into it with her, but I didn't want to lie.

"Yes. Yes, he was bringing it to her."

"Typical," was all she said as the phone clicked.

I hated getting in between my mom and dad. It was a battle I couldn't win. My mom could get so angry, and my dad normally just retreated to his corner.

I started playing with my necklace when suddenly, strong arms encircled me—it was Daniel. He smiled, taking a seat on the bed. He was close. Very close.

I tried to smile back, but it came out like a half grimace. His smile fell and he lifted my chin up so our eyes would meet.

"Tamzin, what's wrong?"

I shrugged, trying to shake off the feeling. "Oh no, it's nothing. I'm fine. Don't worry about it."

"What did I do wrong?"

I chuckled, shaking my head at him. "Why do you assume it's you? You never do anything besides be there for me when I need you. Literally. You always come when I 'summon' you." I actually made air quotes because I wasn't really sure what to call it when he visited.

"Just making sure. If you didn't want me here, I would leave right away."

"No, no, no! Having you around always makes me feel better."

"Okay, then. So if it's not me," he said with an exaggerated long breath of air, wiping at his forehead, "then what is it?"

"It's nothing. Seriously, it's whatever. I don't really want to talk about it right now."

"Okay, I'm not going to push you. But I do hope you know that it's not nothing if it's keeping your wonderful face from smiling. If you need to talk to me about something important, I will make the time for you. Always."

"I mean, what else would you do with your time if you didn't have me around?" I stuck my tongue out at him, but grabbed his

61

hand and squeezed it so he knew that I was grateful to have him around. He put his arm around me, and I rested my head on his shoulder. We sat like that, reveling in the silence and the proximity of our bodies for a few minutes.

Finally, I said, "It's my parents." It came out so quietly that I didn't think he would hear me.

He seemed to contemplate something for a few seconds, then said, "Are they not doing well?"

"They've just been fighting, and I can't deal with their relationship problems on top of everything else I have on my mind right now. Like, I literally can't deal with all of this. I think I'm going to explode one of these days."

"You don't think..."

I knew exactly what he was going to say. "No, they won't get a divorce. It's nothing like that, but still. It's just too much to deal with right now."

"I know that things have been hard, but you're stronger than anyone I've ever met. Things will get easier, I promise," he said, stroking the flyaway hairs at the top of my head.

"Thank you." I paused, train of thought shifting to Daniel and his situation. "Hey, we should go down to the station on Wednesday when I get out of school. I know that Joe wants to see you and my mom will be back at the office... Maybe she can help?"

Daniel got a faraway look, like all of a sudden the weight of his reality was finally crashing on top of him. He squeezed my shoulder, but I could feel his hand trembling. "That sounds good," he said, practically whispering.

"If you're not ready to look into this, you don't have to. It's okay to be scared."

"I'm worried... Worried because I don't know what will happen when we solve my murder."

"I know. Me, too."

My heart went out to him. I knew this wasn't easy, to truly face the fact that he's not only dead but that he was killed. I couldn't even wrap my brain around that. And I couldn't even think that he might be gone forever if he does get closure.

I gave him a hug because I didn't know what to say. Nothing that I could say would change his situation, so I think that not speaking was more appropriate in this case. He wrapped his arms around me, clearing his throat as if he was trying not to cry. Could ghosts cry?

10

I woke up refreshed. Maybe Daniel somehow made the dreams go away? Looking beside me, I almost wished he was still here. I looked over at the cymbal monkey perched on my desk.

"Hi, Beans," I said, not expecting a response.

"Hello, Tamzin!" Beans replied.

I still felt crazy talking to him, since nobody else was able to hear him, but I was glad that he actually responded.

"I'll be back up in a few minutes, okay?"

"Yes. I am Beans!"

I smiled at him as I stretched and got out from under the warm blankets. I sensed something was wrong—or, rather that something was missing. I didn't smell any pancakes. Uh oh... I hoped I had enough time to make a quick breakfast. It might just be a protein bar today.

I shuffled downstairs, not smelling any coffee either. It was rare that my dad didn't have a pot brewing. I didn't miss the smell, though, since I didn't like coffee. I poked my head in the kitchen, but Dad was nowhere to be seen. I tried the intercom linked to the *Dungeon of Curious Oddities*.

"Dad? Dad, are you down there?"

I waited a few seconds, then decided to check his room. I couldn't remember the last time I woke up and my dad was still in bed. I knocked on his door, then quietly let myself in. There was a bundle of something under the covers. I softly poked it and got a *Mrhmhm* in response. He was still in bed?

This was so out of character for him. "Dad, are you okay? You slept in..."

"Mrhmhm... yeah."

"Do you want me to make you something to eat?"

"No. I'm set."

"Okay, Dad. I'm grabbing a power bar and heading off to school. I love you."

"Mrhmhm…" Then I heard snoring.

I shook my head and headed out of his room, quietly closing the door behind me. Maybe he needed some extra sleep. Running back upstairs, I grabbed my backpack and noticed that Beans was now sitting on my bed.

"Beans scared."

"Why are you scared?"

"You shouldn't help the bad lady."

"I'm not sure I understand, Beans."

"The dark hair woman. She is bad. Very bad. I see her at night."

"Where do you see her?"

"In the dark lands with fire. Beans scared. Please don't help her!"

I really didn't know what he was talking about, but I didn't have time if I wanted to make it to class.

"Okay, Beans. I won't help her."

"I am Beans!"

I gave him a hug, hoping to calm him down, and kissed him on the cheek. I gently put him back down on my bed and headed out.

~

"Jimmy, can you hand me the stapler?" We were stopped at a wooden pole that was already plastered with flyers. Jimmy was carrying the stuff to hang the ads, and I had the posters for Mayor Turner.

Jimmy gave me the stapler and took one of the posters out of my hand as I stapled a flyer to the post.

"Yumi Turner for Mayor. The Woman Who Will Bring Change to Our State," Jimmy read in a singsong voice, looking from the poster to me, raising his eyebrows. "Is she for real? This sounds so… cliché."

"I mean, everyone's gotta have some kind of slogan, though, right? I guess it's okay for her to be cliché as long as it works."

"You don't actually support her, do you? I mean, like you're just doing this to say you helped the mayor?"

"Well no, I'm not just doing this as something to put on my resume. She asked for my help, so I wanted to be there for her."

"Right, got it." Even though I agreed with him about Mayor Turner's slogan and how helping the mayor would look good, something about the way he said it made me upset. I was working for Mayor Turner, so I wanted to do my best to help her and stay positive about her campaign. I was beginning to regret asking him to come... We weren't always seeing eye to eye these days.

Even though his comment bothered me, I tried to brush it off. We were out together, so I didn't want to ruin that. And he was helping me when he didn't have to. I always appreciated him and everything he did for me.

I snatched the poster from his hand and gently hit him in the arm with the stapler, motioning for him to take it back.

He scoffed at me. "I was reading that you know! People nowadays."

"I know, right? What are we going to do with them?"

"Who knows."

"Well, what I do know is that you're supposed to be carrying this stapler." I smiled, holding the stapler out for him to take. He took it without protest, putting his arm around me as we walked down the sidewalk.

"I'm glad you asked me to come help."

I nodded, feeling guilty for being upset with him. I had no idea what I wanted anymore. We continued posting the flyers until we ran out. The weather was nice, which made the walk enjoyable, but I was still confused about Jimmy. Daniel was making his way into my heart, which made my time with Jimmy not as much fun as it used to be.

~

I was standing in front of the Springfield Science Museum. It was an old building, and I'm pretty sure it was originally a large gothic cathedral. It had a huge courtyard that extended to either

66

side. A few decades ago, most of the large, wrought iron fence had been removed, leaving the gate which opened to the middle walkway that led to the front entrance. I wasn't sure why the gate had been left, since it served no purpose, but it was pretty. The gothic building itself was also beautiful, especially since its facade had been well maintained.

It was about four blocks from where the Puritan Theatre had been—where the whole battle with Jack the Ripper went down. Now, that area was just a cavernous hole surrounded by a fence. *Insanity*, I thought.

Walking through the gate, I moved to the front entrance. One door was held open, so I went in. I felt the cool breeze brush against my skin as I went through the anteroom and walked up to the main desk.

"Hi," I said to the woman at the desk.

"Oh, hello. How are you, young lady? It's five dollars to enter the exhibit hall today."

She peered at me over her glasses. I thought about trying to get out of paying the fee, but then figured it would be fruitless. I reached into my purse and pulled out the cash.

"Here you go."

"Thank you, dear. Here is a map and some coupons for local establishments."

I took a brief glance at the things she gave me and noticed the Puritan Theatre symbol. I guess they had been an advertiser prior to the collapse.

"One question. Can you tell me where I can find Miral Nefertari?"

The woman stopped cold, almost frozen in place. Her mouth opened as if to answer, then it closed. It opened again, then closed. She kept repeating this over and over again while the rest of her body was stuck in place. The thing that creeped me out the most was that her eyes focused on me, but as I moved they stayed in place. I took another step to the side, but she didn't budge, other than her mouth slowly opening and closing.

A group of students came through the door with their teacher and a few aides. The woman at the counter snapped out of it.

"Can I help you?" she asked the teacher. The kids milled about as the aides tried to herd them together. I took this moment to leave, deciding to find Miral on my own.

The main lobby held an awesome t-rex skeleton. Pam was her name. Majestic but terrifying if you thought of her when she was alive. As I walked by, the children started surrounding her as they oohed and aahed.

I looked at the map of the exhibits. Behind the large room enclosing the Egyptian artifacts was the entrance to the curator's room for antiquities. It didn't mention the *Mummy Extravaganza*, but I hoped this was where Miral might be.

I passed by a number of glass enclosed items from various pyramids and excavations. They were beautiful. Gold coverings, gemstone adornments, intricate carvings—embellishments on pottery, dishes, weapons and every manner of thing possible. I'd normally stop to read about their history, but today I was on a mission.

I found a back door. I surmised this was the room with the new antiquities as it was guarded by a very large man in a security guard outfit. His nametag said "Ron".

"Hi, Ron. How are you?"

"I'm good, ma'am. Can I help you?"

"Yes, I'm looking for Miral Nefertari?"

Bam! He froze just like the woman at the front desk. I waved my hand in front of his face.

"Ma'am, what are you doing?"

Oops, I guess he was just standing very still...

"Miral, is she behind door number 3?"

"Visitors to the museum are not allowed in the curator's sections."

"Could you let her know I'm here? My name is Tamzin Clarke."

"Ms. Clarke? Is your father Thomas Clarke?"

"Yeah. He's my dad."

He didn't say another word as he reached for his keycard. He swiped it, then put in a code. The door made a noise and popped open.

"Thank you, sir."

"You're welcome, your highness."

I did a double take at that comment but hopped through the door before he could change his mind. *Your highness...* I could get used to that.

Walking into the room, I had a very strong feeling of déjà vu. The boxes and crates, the strewn packing materials, the cluttered tables—all were exactly like they were in my dreams. The hairs on the back of my neck stood up, seeming to say "please, leave now!" Other than the déjà vu and my hair sticking up, I didn't feel the need to leave. I heard some voices from the back and headed toward them.

At first, I made out a man and woman's voice. Then, I realized that the woman was Miral. The man sounded upset, but he wasn't totally enraged.

"...can't be put outside. How did you even come up with that idea?"

"I know it's unorthodox, Mr. Miller, but I believe it will make a spectacular advertisement for *Mummy Extravaganza*."

"Yes, it would. But, I'm worried about the fragility of some of the pieces."

"I understand—" Miral said as she turned and looked to me. "Well, hello Tamzin."

Mr. Miller was older, bald with white hair. He looked like an administrator, but I wasn't sure.

"Mr. Miller, this is Tamzin Clarke, the daughter of Thomas Clarke who has helped us put together the final pieces of our exhibit."

"Oh, yes. I also know that you helped with that serial killer," he said as he came over to shake my hand.

"I really didn't do much—"

"Oh, nonsense. Your father bragged about you for hours. It sounds as if you were the only person to even understand how crazy the Ripper was, well, before we knew he was the Ripper."

"Uhm, I guess." He continued to shake my hand. It wasn't uncomfortable, though, because he seemed genuinely happy to meet me, almost like I was a celebrity.

"Okay... I will let you two have your meeting. Ms. Nefertari, we will continue our discussion later. I do not believe I can allow what you are asking, though," Mr. Miller said, giving a curt nod.

With that, he left me with Miral. She looked at me very calmly. After a moment, I realized that she was wondering why I was here. I wasn't sure why she didn't say anything, though.

"Miral... can you tell me more about the exhibit?" I wasn't really sure what to do or say. I guess I would make it up as I went along and see if something made sense with all of this mummy stuff.

"Well... the first thing to know is that we are featuring a new dig which was championed by this museum. I helped put together the financing and was on hand for much of the work. The tomb is believed to be that of Amenhotep the second. He was a ruling pharaoh of the eighteenth dynasty in Egypt."

My heart skipped about five beats. Amenhotep? That was the name of the prince from my dreams. The *Mummy Extravaganza* should really be called *Mummy Madness* because this was one crazy coincidence. I felt a bit light headed, and took a slight step back, almost falling. Miral reached forward to steady me. As her hand grabbed my arm, it was like a jolt of electricity ran between us. We both immediately locked eyes, cocking our heads and furrowing our brows. It would have been funny since we were subconsciously mimicking each other, but I had a massive sense of déjà vu.

I felt like something was wrong with her—like her aura had changed from when I had first met her.

She let go of my arm and the feeling stopped. We both stood up straight and studied each other. I had no idea what was going through her head, but mine was one big question mark.

She was the first to recover, saying, "Your dad is coming over later to help."

"Oh, cool. I know he's been excited working on this project. He seems glad to be working with you, too, since you were college friends."

"We were much more than friends..." She got a far away look. I must have had a nauseous expression on my face because I knew what she was implying. I decided that now was the time to leave.

"I don't think I needed to know that. I better get back home. Thank you for talking with me."

"No problem. And, please say hi to your dad for me," she said, cocking her head and smiling. She could have been the cat that caught the canary.

~

I was sitting on the couch in the living room, trying to figure out what to do with myself. It wasn't normal for me to be home alone, so this kind of freedom felt weird. I was playing around with my phone when I heard someone coming through the door. I jumped, almost dropping my phone on the floor.

I saw Nomi first, followed by my mom. Nomi kept looking back at her to make sure she was okay.

"Nomi, please. I'm fine." Nomi put her hands up in defense, walking further into the house. Mom shut the door behind her, then they both noticed me. I jumped up and ran over to give my mom a gentle squeeze. It was nice to see her back home.

She let out a pained sigh and said, "Not too tight, Tam. I'm not fully recovered around the ribs yet."

Maybe I wasn't as gentle as I thought. I quickly moved my arms away, cringing. "Oh God, I'm sorry."

"No, it's okay. It's good to see my little girl." She smiled at me, stroking the hair at the top of my head.

Nomi walked over to me, giving me a hug. She seemed to start when she touched me but kept her voice calm and conversational. "Tam, my girl. How are you?" When she pulled away, she looked concerned and a bit confused, like she had sensed something, but then she smiled.

"I'm doing pretty good. Even better now that I get to see both of you."

"Wonderful, wonderful. Your mom wasn't even supposed to be out yet, but they let me take her a day early with some persuasion on my end." Nomi winked at me, and I couldn't help but wonder if she used some sort of her witchy voodoo on the hospital staff. Mom laughed, shaking her head.

"I can always count on Nomi to break me out."

"Darling, I think they wanted you gone. You weren't exactly the most cooperative patient. But hey, that's the spirit that gives your aura its fiery color."

Mom rolled her eyes behind Nomi's back. She still had trouble believing in the mystical, even after the whole fiasco with Jack the Ripper. I even questioned that kind of stuff sometimes, too.

"Tam, girl, where's your father? I want to say hello."

Mom let out a sarcastic laugh, going toward the fridge. She pulled out a bottle of wine and got a wine glass from the cupboard. "Of course he's not home. He never even came to visit me. He's been busy with all of his *work*." She popped the top off of the bottle and filled the entire glass.

Nomi raised her eyebrows at me, and I shrugged. "Maybe it's best if I be going now. I'm glad you're finally out of that hospital, Irene. You know how I hate those places. Be well my friends."

And with that, Nomi left us alone. She sat on the couch, pinching the bridge of her nose as if she had a headache.

"Maybe you should just go to sleep, Mom. I'm sure you're exhausted."

"I will soon. I want to wait for your dad to come home."

Uh oh, I knew this wasn't going to be good. I sat down on the couch with her, hoping that having me around would help her feel a little better. I put the TV on and looked for a movie that we could watch together.

About an hour later, I was just starting to doze off when the door opened. It was Dad.

"Where have you been?" Mom asked, putting her empty wine glass down on the counter.

Dad gave her an unamused look, not answering her question. He took off his shoes and coat, slowly making his way toward the staircase.

"Excuse me, I asked you a question," she said, voice rising. "I bet you were with *her*, weren't you?"

Dad clenched his fists, then unclenched them. He kept doing that over and over again.

"Couldn't even visit me in the damn hospital. I am your wife! Not her."

"Irene!" Dad yelled, gripping the railing of the staircase until his knuckles turned white. Mom and I both jumped, looking at each other. All of the color drained out of Mom's face. Dad never yelled. Never. "I am *not* getting into this with you right now. Stop being so petty." With that, he walked up the stairs to go to bed.

Mom and I just sat there, stunned. What was going on?

11

Daniel and I were walking up the steps of the Police Headquarters. I was hesitant to go back to the place where my mom had been stabbed and nearly killed, but she's since healed and was back—as Chief of Police. Large and in charge!

I hadn't seen my dad this morning. I wasn't sure what was up with him, but I hoped that my parents would work out their differences. Before Miral came back into the picture, everything was going well. Er... I guess. My mom and dad had their moments, but I knew that they truly loved each other. They weren't living together only because of me. They had a relationship that allowed them to feed off the other's strengths. Even though they were basically opposites, they still clicked and made a good pair.

We entered the large glass doors, walking past the front desk. The interior was still being renovated after Jack's onslaught. Many spots were covered up, but where there was exposed concrete, I noticed a number of bullet dings and holes. They were still bringing in pieces of glass to replace the originals—I think every single window on this entire floor had been shattered.

Joe was waiting at the head of the hallway, waving us over.

"Hey, guys. Let's check in on your mom first. She's settling into her new office. It's on the third floor, so it didn't need repairs."

He awkwardly leaned down to hug Daniel, who reciprocated with a big hug back. Daniel seemed to have gotten over his concerns about Joe and was not afraid to show his love. I could see Joe's face light up, tension loosening from around his eyes.

"I hope we have somethin' that can help figure this out. No matter what, I'm just glad to have you back. I wish our mom and dad lived to see you... but I guess they must already know."

This thought seemed to buoy Joe as he ushered us down to the elevators. The hallway still needed a lot of work, and the door to the holding cells hung on its hinges, twisted metal banged into an obscene work of modern art.

"I don't think your mother knows you're here today."

"Yeah, things were pretty crazy after she came home from the hospital. I don't think I mentioned it. Hopefully we'll catch her at a good time." What I was really thinking was *catch her in a good mood*.

Exiting the elevator, we headed down another hallway. I could see "Chief of Police" on a plaque outside the door facing us. Unlike most of the doors on the first floor, this one was made of ornate wood and was extra large. Joe knocked on the door.

"Hey, Irene, it's me, Joe. Got Tamzin and my brother here, too."

We didn't hear a response, so Joe poked his head in. He waved us over, silencing us with a finger over his lips.

"She's on the phone," he whispered.

We snuck in. She looked like she was in work mode, but I didn't sense any hostility. I caught her grimacing as she hung up the phone—most likely pain from the broken ribs and punctured lung.

"Hi, Chief. Got the youth patrol here."

"Hey, Joe. No need to call me Chief, at least not when we are alone."

I went around the desk to give my mom a hug.

"Did you see your father this morning?"

I studied her before answering. I didn't really get a read on any emotions coming from her, no anger or positivity.

"I had to rush to school. Not sure if Dad was even awake. Since he wasn't feeling well, I didn't want to wake him if he needed sleep."

"Okay. We can talk about your dad later..."

She looked up and locked eyes on Joe. He seemed worried but shook it off.

"Yes, Boss?"

"Detective Berkowski, since your family is here it might be a good time to say this," she said, gesturing to Daniel. "I wanted to offer you a promotion to Captain."

75

Joe stepped back, rubbing his head. "Wow... I didn't expect to ever be promoted to Captain."

"So... what do you think?"

"Absolutely!"

"Yeah!" Daniel said as he grabbed Joe's hand for a hearty shake.

"Congratulations, Joe!" I offered, also shaking his hand.

"I'll still need you to finish off your current cases. And occasionally fill in until we are back up to full staff. Are you okay with that?"

"Sure. Whatever you need, I'm there. We still have a lot of work to do."

"Yes," she said, offering her hand. "Captain Joseph Berkowski, I welcome you to your new rank!"

Mom came around and gave him a hug. I think I saw a tear run down Joe's cheek. She pulled away, and it almost looked like she was crying, too.

"Oh, Joe, I had the file clerk send up that dossier you had requested. I told him to get it in your new office, two doors down from me."

"Thank you, Irene." He stood there looking at her, not sure what to do.

"Okay, off to work. Keep me posted on anything you find about Daniel's case."

"I will."

We turned and headed out. Two doors down, Joe stood in front of the door with "Captain" emboldened on it. He seemed shocked, in awe of his new title, but then grasped the handle and walked in. This office was pretty empty, no papers or other knick knacks, but it had a large desk with a chair, two bookshelves, and a small square table that looked as if it could act as a place to have a four-person conference or a four-person lunch. On the table was a large folder that Joe picked up. He started leafing through the pages inside.

"It was a long time ago, so these files aren't on the computer." He kept flipping the pages, occasionally letting out a grunt or a *hmmm*.

"This may take a while…" We all sat down as he sifted through more pages. "I'm kinda hungry. How's about I hop down to the cafeteria and see if there's anything that resembles food, okay? I will grab something for all of us. You guys can look through these docs. Since they are so old, I don't think anyone would care."

"Cool, Joe, sounds good," I said, desperate to get something to eat.

"Okay, I'll be back in a few…"

He headed out and Daniel and I split the papers between us.

"Thanks, Tamzin. I really appreciate you helping with this."

"Eh, it's no problem. I want to figure out what happened to you. And, once we solve the mystery…"

I immediately realized this was not a good subject. We both assumed that when Daniel solved the mystery of his death, he would go into the light, meaning we would no longer be able to see each other. I think he realized my train of thought.

"Yeah, it's a bummer. I don't want to leave you. I finally feel 'complete' with you, but when the killer is revealed, I will head off to wherever that light takes me."

"I know. Well, let's take our time. Your murderer might be dead now. Well, maybe."

"I don't know… Yep, let's find out *slowly*." He looked at me and wiggled his eyebrows. I playfully pushed his shoulder, laughing.

I continued ruffling through my pages when I came across something.

"Look. It's a report on another girl who went missing the day after you did. That's a coincidence."

"Yes, yes it is."

"Her name was Angie Santiago. She was sixteen. She had told her mom she was heading down to the river where you think you were killed. Do you remember her?"

"No. I can't remember anything from before I woke up on the beach."

"There is only one sheet on her. There's a copier in my mom's office."

77

We headed over, but Mom was gone. We made a quick copy and went back to Joe's new office. He came up to the door just as we got back.

"Any luck with the reports?"

"We found one thing. Just made a copy. It's another girl who had disappeared."

"Oh, yeah, I remember her. She went to the same high school we did—where you go now, Tamzin. She was never found, either. There was a lot of talk that you two had gone off together, but I didn't buy it. You were my big brother, and you wouldn't leave me."

"Do you remember anything else about her?"

"Not really. She was Hispanic and kept to her group. We were less integrated back then and crossing race boundaries was more taboo."

"Hmmm... and she was never found?"

"Nope. Not that I recall. I did another search when I got on the force and was able to review the documents. I looked for her on our databases and nothin' came up. I can run one now since we are more hooked into the state and fed. Maybe there's something new."

"Okay, sounds good. We can search for her on our computers, also."

We sat down and ate some of the food Joe had brought up. I'm still not sure what it was, but it didn't taste too bad.

~

The audience was buzzing with excitement, waiting for Vanessa to come on stage. The rest of the band members were out testing their instruments, including Jimmy. He looked good tonight, wearing a blue t-shirt that really brought out his eyes. He didn't look down and smile at me like he usually did before a performance, but I had just assumed he was concentrating on getting his stuff set up and kind of forgot that we were all here. He could get lost in his music, and when he was in his playing mindset, it was like no one else was in the room.

Even though I've been confused about Jimmy lately, I was still disappointed that he didn't give me that smile. I almost felt like it was his way of telling me that he didn't care anymore, and that fact hurt more than anything else. I tried not to think about any of that, though. I just wanted to focus on the music and the atmosphere of the place.

The Rivoli was relatively small, so it was perfect for tonight's event. There were about forty people in the audience, which was a pretty good turn out for something like this.

I was sitting with Tony and Macy in the front row. They were sitting close to each other, laughing at something they shared between the two of them, and I noticed that their feet were entwined below the seats.

I gave Macy a look, raising my eyebrows when Tony turned his back to me. She opened her mouth to protest, but couldn't help but smile. I rolled my eyes at her, shifting in my seat so I could focus on the stage.

The lights dimmed and Vanessa walked out, clad in all black. She was wearing a lot of makeup and wore the highest heels I had ever seen, but she didn't look trashy. She commanded the stage from the second she walked out, drawing everyone's attention toward her.

Right when she came out, Tony let out a loud whistle. "Ow, ow! Babe alert," he said, tongue practically hanging out.

"Tony, settle down," Macy said, resting her hand on his shoulder, gripping it slightly harder than she should have. Even though she sounded relatively calm, I could tell that she was getting jealous. In fact, she looked absolutely pissed right now. The expression on her face was anything but pleasant. Tony was so clueless sometimes...

"Hello," Vanessa drawled into the microphone. She was standing at the center of the stage, tapping her foot to the beat of whatever song was in her head. "I want to thank all of you for coming out tonight. I want y'all to give a big round of applause for the boys who got my back. I'm honored to have been chosen as the singer for this rockin' band."

We all started clapping, with the exception of Tony who decided to snap instead.

"Good form, Tony. Good form," I said, attempting to snap along with him. He started going faster and faster, and his snaps were getting louder and louder. He was definitely snapping louder than me, but at least I tried.

When the audience finally quieted down, Tony kept snapping for *way* longer than he should have, and the band started playing. From the second Vanessa opened her mouth, no one could look away. Her voice was so amazing, smooth as honey, and having a rocking band behind her only helped amplify her skill.

They kept going into song after song, and it was obvious that the audience was having a great time. You could tell that everyone on the stage was feeling it, too. For me, it was also nice to be here with Tony and Macy, even if they were practically on a date.

When they finished up with their next song, Vanessa took a sip of water, flipping her hair and swinging her hips. "Okay, my lovelies. I hate to say it, but we only have one song left. Let's make it the best one yet!"

They started playing and everyone got on their feet to dance. Vanessa was gyrating as she belted out the tune, moving in perfect rhythm to the beat. Tony grabbed Macy by the waist and pulled her over to dance. I was standing next to them, moving my hips to the music. I could feel the energy of everyone in the room, and it was contagious. I really wanted to grab a random stranger and start dancing with them. Of course, I would never do that, but the mere thought of it was exciting.

Just as the song was finishing, I could have sworn Vanessa looked me right in the eye and winked. Everything after that seemed to go in slow motion, like whatever happened was too much for my mind to process in the heat of the moment.

Vanessa made her way, very seductively, over to Jimmy, swinging her hips as she went. She draped her arm over his shoulder, rubbing her hand up and down his chest. She was still singing and he was still playing, so it seemed like it was mostly friendly and part of the act. But, right as the song ended, Vanessa grabbed Jimmy by the shirt and kissed him. Her lips went right to his lips. It was hard to see him, but I'm pretty sure he looked as shocked as I was. Time literally seemed to stand still. My mouth was wide open and I put my hands over it to cover up my surprise and anger.

I pushed my way through the crowd to get out of there as quickly as possible. I could feel the tears stinging my eyes, and I felt like I was going to puke. I didn't even look back.

12

Once again, I was lurking in the shadows. I could hear voices—what sounded like arguing—close by. I moved toward the sounds and realized they were Miral and Mr. Miller, the administrator of the museum.

"You can't put any of the exhibit items outside, even if it's for advertising. One bad storm and we risk damage."

"I think this is very important to get the people we need."

"I don't even know how the security and museum staff unions will respond. We'd need around the clock security details outside. They'll probably strike because they will melt if it rains!"

"Mr. Miller, you know I have great respect for you. This, though, is no longer your decision."

She looked directly at me as I came out from behind some crates. The administrator looked up at me, his eyes showing familiarity at first. As I got closer, his eyes bulged, and he stepped back, putting his arms up in defense.

My arm shot up and pointed at him, making a fist. Like before, I cringed when I saw the exposed bone and rotting flesh. Ancient wraps were hanging off my forearm. I felt a surge of energy directed at Miller as he clawed at his neck, trying to loosen his collar.

Angry red spots appeared on his face. They bulged out into pus-filled sores. As they grew larger, he began to tear at his flesh, screaming with each piece of torn skin. The pustules exploded and greyish ooze ran down his face. He started tearing at his clothes, attempting to scratch at the boils underneath. He tore open his shirt revealing a mass of twisted flesh.

He fell to his knees, looking up at Miral with a pained expression. He opened his mouth to speak, but only blood spilled out. With a final gasp, he fell to the floor. Miral laughed as his body spasmed.

I woke up gagging, trying to keep last night's dinner down. I knew that couldn't be Miral in my vision—there was no way. From the few times I've interacted with her, I gathered that she definitely couldn't be that twisted. It was almost as if she was a different person in the nightmare. I tried to push the images away. Oh well... I'd better get ready for school.

~

I was sitting in the media room on the second floor, eating lunch by myself. I've felt like an outsider lately, and I didn't have the guts to face my friends or eat alone in a crowded cafeteria. Jimmy and I were... well, I don't know what was going on with us, and I had no idea where our relationship was heading. Tony and Macy were essentially a thing, so they really only paid attention to each other. And beyond them, I didn't have anyone else at school. The only time I felt "whole" was when I was with Daniel. But being with a ghost wasn't exactly practical.

I took a bite of my salad, trying to relax and forget about all of the drama. This room had a wall of floor to ceiling windows. The curtains were open, and the view was nice—over the valley, with Springfield on the other side. The sun shone, not a cloud in sight. Sometimes, just being alone with nature could make anyone feel better.

I focused on my salad, then had a jello cup for dessert. It wasn't very good, but it was one of the more edible things offered for lunch. Finishing up, I noticed that some clouds had formed. Wow, that was fast. They coalesced over the city center and looked threatening. I jumped when a blast of lightning and the sound of thunder struck. Our school wasn't far from the cloud formation.

I stood, mesmerized in a way, as the clouds whirled around in a frenzy. Lightning kept flashing between the clouds and the area grew larger but stayed centered where it was.

The media room door slammed open, and I jumped. It was just a freshman that must have been in the AV Club. He pulled up a remote and turned on one of the TVs. I had no idea why he was in here, probably just to look at the news, but I didn't really mind. Dan

Defino's head was prominent on the screen, which read "Weather Advisory".

"The Storm Team is issuing a local weather advisory. A freak storm has formed above Springfield," he said, pausing for effect. "Winds in excess of forty miles per hour have been recorded."

I looked at the freshman. He seemed scared, but I could tell that he was trying to look like he didn't care.

"Please stay indoors if possible and tune in for updates as the day progresses." He looked down at his pile of papers and continued. "Also, please remember to contact our station or the police if you hear any word on the St. Stephen's Academy school children. A class visiting the Springfield Science Museum disappeared on their way back to school. Federal officials have stepped in to help since our local police department is still reeling from their recent losses."

The clouds appeared very dense as they swirled with the spouts of wind. Small thunderbolts were almost non-stop, with huge bolts blasting every minute or so. Thunderclaps followed suit, one of them shaking our building. Wow, this was intense. With that thought, the intercom sounded.

"Students, we are closing the school for the remainder of the day. Please stay indoors until your bus or ride is here. We will be gathering in the cafeteria in the meantime. Once again, the school is officially closed. Do not head outdoors until your ride is here. This storm is very dangerous."

The young student looked worried.

"Hey, let's go down to the cafeteria together, okay?"

He nodded and we walked out. He reached out cautiously, like he wasn't sure how I would react, and I grabbed his hand—I needed to be the strong one, keep him from freaking out. And, yeah, I admit that having another person with me made me feel a little safer.

~

Since the bizarre weather had gotten us sent home from school, I decided to take that time to further our investigation into

Daniel's death. I started looking online, trying to get more information on the girl that disappeared when Daniel had. I didn't find much, especially since it was several years ago, but I did manage to find her old address. And, it looked like her family still owned the home.

Further investigation found little else that had happened that day, at least for stuff that was recorded online. They did list a full moon, a power outage, and a bunch of stolen cars. Even though these details seemed insignificant, I wanted to gather as much information as possible. Maybe some pieces would fit together to solve the mystery...

I thought about Daniel, touching my necklace, and waited for him to show up. I laughed to myself, thinking of all the different things I could title the way I summon him. I was so lost in thought that the sound of his voice made me jump.

"Why are you giggling?" Daniel asked.

"I was just trying to think of a good name for how I get in touch with you. At first, I thought 'the dragonfly signal', but that's too long and nowhere near cool enough."

"Hmmm... How about 'the dragon summon'?"

"Better... Still wordy, though."

"Dragon's call?"

"Not bad. I'll keep that one in mind."

He chuckled, shaking his head at me. "So, what's up?"

"Nothing too serious, but I did find the address of that girl that went missing. Her family still owns the house. Since I'm out of school, I was thinking maybe we could head over?"

"Uhm, sure... As long as it's not too close to the storm. That thing looks crazy."

"Yeah. I was watching it from school and it looked really bad, and I wasn't even close to it."

We headed out, hoping to find something. Even though the timing was close, I wasn't sure that her disappearance had anything to do with Daniel.

~

The address was 1428 Elm Street, close to the end of the road. Walking down the sidewalk, it basically looked like all the other Queen Anne type homes in the neighborhood. They were kind of cool, and most places in this area of town were well maintained. As we walked up to the front door, I wasn't sure what to do.

"What should we say?" I asked Daniel.

"Uhm... I don't know. Maybe make something up?"

"I don't want to lie."

"Yeah, but telling them a ghost is interested in finding out what happened to their family member many years ago probably won't cut it."

"Yeah... You're right. I'll try to come up with something."

The door had a large metal knocker. I clanged it three times, and we waited. After a few moments, a young girl answered.

"Hello," I said.

"Hello." She looked us up and down, scrunching her nose.

"We were wondering if we could talk to an adult? Someone who may have been around a few decades ago?"

Her face softened, and she looked back as if she wasn't sure if she should let us in or not, then said, "I can get Gramma. Come in."

We walked from the foyer to the living room. It was basically what I had expected, with pictures adorning the walls and mantle.

"Tamzin. Look at this!"

Daniel was holding a picture frame from one of the tables at the back of the room. On the table were pictures of one girl in particular. Looking more closely, I recognized her—Angie Santiago. The picture that Daniel was holding proved to be even more useful. I saw that the girl was in it, but she was clinging to a boy. And there was no mistaking that it was Daniel...

"Can I help you, two?"

I nearly jumped as an elderly woman came up behind us.

"Hi. My name is Tamzin Clarke. We were looking for information on Angie Santiago? We were looking to—"

The woman froze, staring at Daniel. She slowly walked up to him, inspecting his face. "My gosh. You are the spitting image of Angie's boyfriend! He disappeared with her."

My mind was reeling at this bit of information. How did Daniel have no recollection of his *girlfriend*?

Daniel and I exchanged a look, silently agreeing that we wouldn't tell her anything she shouldn't know.

"Uhm… Hi. My name is John. You must be referring to Daniel? He was a relative of mine and we are trying to get more information on his disappearance."

"My, my. I can't believe how similar you look. If that weren't many years ago, I'd swear that you were him. He was a very nice boy."

"Are you Angie's mother?" he asked.

"Yes. I lost my daughter. We never found anything at all. For many years, I assumed that the two of you ran off. Oh, I'm sorry, I mean that she and Daniel had run off. After not hearing anything for so long, I gave up hope."

"Do you have any other information that could help us?" I asked.

"I have tried to put it out of my mind, but I do have an old scrapbook from when she was alive. I kept clippings from the newspaper stories that I thought might be linked to her after she had disappeared, but nothing ever came of them."

"Would you mind if we looked at the book? It might have something…" I didn't want to push her, but we needed to get the information somehow.

"Yes. I have no use for it anymore. But, I do want you to tell me if you find anything concrete. Otherwise, I need to keep it behind me."

She walked back up the stairs, and the young girl who answered the door came down.

"Hello."

"Hi, little one," I said, kneeling down to talk at her eye level.

"My name is Angela. I was named after my aunt. I think you said that you are going to look for her?"

"Yes, we are going to try."

Daniel looked at all the pictures displayed on the table intensely. I knew he was trying to remember something, but it seemed like he was drawing a blank.

"My mommy gets sad when she thinks about Angie. She missed her a lot when she went away."

"Well, hopefully we can figure out what happened. Maybe that will make your mom feel better."

"I hope so. When she's happy she gives me candy."

"Candy is always a good thing." I smiled at her.

"I like chocolate, too. Candy and chocolate."

Angela was almost as cute as Max.

"Here it is," Gramma said, handing me a very large scrapbook. There were pages hanging out with folded news articles. She definitely put a lot of time into finding information. I just hope that there was something useful in here.

"Thank you very much. You are so kind to let us have the book."

"Well, as I said, I've put it behind me. Too much pain for me to think about it anymore. I gave away too much of my life as it was."

"Gramma, can I have some chocolate?"

"Well, since you've been good, I think you deserve some chocolate. Maybe I'll sneak a piece, too." She winked at Angela, then gestured to me and Daniel. "Would you both like some?"

"I'm okay, ma'am," Daniel said, nodding at her.

"Me, too. We should get on our way, especially with this crazy storm and all."

"Yes. Please be careful going home. I don't know what to think of that storm. I've never seen anything like it."

"We will. Thank you. And nice meeting both of you," I said.

"Yes, many thanks," said Daniel. He seemed off, I'm sure this wasn't easy for him, but it was good that we found out that he was dating that girl.

We walked to the door, with Gramma and Angela following suit. When we were on the sidewalk heading home, I noticed them waving from the doorway. I could hear some of what they were saying to each other, the final word being an excited, "Chocolate!" said in unison.

13

I was following the princess and soon-to-be queen. She crept down the stairs and tiptoed up to the prince's brother's sleeping chambers. After she knocked quickly three times, the boy opened the door and pulled her inside.

I had no access to his room, so I waited patiently in the hall. I was beginning to fall asleep when they dashed out. Fortunately, I was half covered by a tapestry and in shadow. They walked past and headed up to the floor where the prince slept.

I followed behind, careful not to be seen. I hid near the top of the railing as they whispered in the antechamber adjacent to the prince. They looked around for a moment, then I swear I heard giggling. What were they up to?

The boy pulled out a vial—it looked like one of the herbal medicines used by the palace physicians. I remembered the poppy field in the garden. Could it be some type of painkiller? Hatshepsut pulled out the morning wine for the prince. She poured the entire bottle of liquid into his glass. Poison!

I couldn't watch this any longer—I had to stop them. Defiantly walking in, I grabbed the poisoned drink and threw it to the ground. I wound my hand back and slapped the priestess as hard as I could.

"How could you poison him? You are married!"

"He is nothing to me. I love his brother. He shall be the high pharaoh!"

"The prince loves you! How could you betray him?"

"He doesn't love me, you fool. He loves YOU!"

For a moment, I was confused. He loved me? I knew that I loved him, but I never expected him to have feelings for me. As I stood there, the priestess grabbed the scarab brooch from my dress. She pulled open the long pin.

"But now, you shall die. And he will die with you!"

She plunged the pin into my heart. My head was still spinning from her talk about love—but now it started spinning as I fell to the floor and left the world of man.

I opened my eyes, feeling pain over my heart. I started to move but realized something was on my neck. Well, I guess you could say snuggling my neck.

"Zzzzz..."

"Beans? Can you wake up?"

"Zzzzz..."

"Beans?"

"Zzzzz..."

"Beans!" I said, raising my voice.

"Mhm. Beans!"

I sat up and held him close. It felt good to have someone to talk to, someone to watch over me. Especially after learning of love, only to get stabbed in the heart.

"Beans saw you were away."

"You mean, dreaming?"

"Beans! I think so."

"Okay... I'm glad you're taking this whole guardian thing seriously."

"Beans do anything for Tamzin. You save Beans!"

"Okay, let's go back to sleep."

"Beans keep bad people away!"

"Good, Beans. Hopefully I won't have a nightmare."

"Zzzzz..."

I laughed and felt my eyes closing as I lay back down.

I was standing directly behind my dad. We were at the science museum, back in the curator's room. Miral was barking orders.

"Take this one out... Now!" She looked at another slave. "No, that one stays here!" She pointed toward a large pedestal. "Yes, that piece goes."

There was a group of people following her commands, and they seemed to be emptying most of the antiquities in the room. As I got a better look at them, I realized that some of the people helping were the students I had seen the other day as well as a group of people that looked like they were in great need of a bath... the homeless that had disappeared?

"Your highness, do you wish me to do anything?" my dad asked, talking to Miral.

"No, not yet. You are going to be my great sacrifice today."

Sacrifice?

"Just stay here while we prepare."

My dad walked to the back of the room, and I followed him. Interestingly enough, my perception of height was about a head taller than I would normally be. It was weird being up higher than my dad. He sat down in a chair in the corner and I noticed a swarm of flies. Looking closer, the rotting bodies of the ambassador and administrator were dumped in a heap in the corner. I don't think I would have been able to breathe if I were actually able to smell.

Miral continued to control the missing people as if they were slaves. Everyone seemed to follow her without hesitation. There was a fair bit of light in the area. I hadn't seen it before, but the ankh was hovering in the center of the room close to the ceiling. It was the same one I had unpacked, the one that seemed to call to me. Maybe it had something to do with all of this?

Miral came over and gestured for us to follow.

"We must begin the ceremony outside."

"Yes, your highness. I give myself to you."

"You do... and after today you will be all mine. Forever."

She turned and walked out, my dad following obediently. A lightbulb went off in my head—the person who looked like Miral must have been Hatshepsut! I don't know why I had this thought, but once I did, things seemed to fall into place and make some kind of sense.

Once again, I awoke with an uneasy feeling. It looked like the sun was just coming up, and I found Beans sitting on the bed, looking my way.

"I am Beans!"

"Yes, I know, Beans. Did you guard me well?"

"Yes."

"I have to get ready for school."

"Tamzin."

"Yes?"

"Dead monkey stops me."

"Dead monkey? Stops you? From what?"

"Beans need to tell you."

"What is it, Beans?"

"Hard to talk."

"Just try. What is it about?"

"Hold my arms."

I held Beans' arms and looked right at him.

"Dead monkey bad. Woman bad. Other woman bad."

I was losing my patience, but I tried to keep it together. After all, I was talking with a cymbal monkey that I had saved from Jack the Ripper.

"Try to concentrate, Beans. I will, too."

Suddenly, I heard the voice of a boy who seemed years older than the normal Beans. And he was very serious.

"It is all real. All of your dreams and visions are true. Your father is in trouble, right NOW!"

I gasped. For some reason, I believed him. Dad was in trouble.

"Beans did it!" He was back to his normal, cute voice.

"Thank you, Beans."

I gave him a hug as I jumped up from the bed. I think it took a lot of his energy because, as I was leaving, I only heard the soft sounds of snoring.

I raced down to my mom's room, knocking feverishly on the door.

"Mom! Mom, Dad is in trouble."

She blearily opened the door.

"I know he is—he never came home. Sleeping at Miral's, no doubt."

"Mom, that's not Miral," I said. I decided to throw my theory out there. "She's been possessed by an ancient Egyptian priestess and is going to sacrifice him."

"What?"

"Now. She's going to sacrifice him *now*!"

If we hadn't been through all the insanity with the demonic Jack the Ripper, I think this conversation would have been over right then and there.

"Okay. Let me get my stuff. Out in sixty seconds."

~

We made it in record time, probably because the streets were empty with this freak storm—or maybe because of Mom's insane driving... She didn't mess around when she needed to be somewhere fast.

We came to a screeching halt outside the museum, with the large gate directly in front of us. In a flash, mom jumped out and had her gun drawn. Following her, I ran through the gate. Bolts of lightning crashed in the clouds, and I realized that the storm was centered over the museum. Thunder boomed and the ground shook so much that I almost lost my balance.

There was a large gathering of people on the lawn, most standing behind Miral and my dad. Scattered throughout the crowd were the missing homeless and the students I had seen the other day. They seemed mesmerized as they knelt down behind Miral and bowed their heads. The sarcophagus sat in front, like an altar, surrounded by four pedestals—each with a canopic jar on top. I recognized the one with the jackal head that contained the stomach.

Miral was chanting, and my dad laid on top of the sarcophagus. She had the ankh attached to a long pole with Egyptian etchings on it. Holding the scepter up, it suddenly glowed bright and momentarily blinded me. Mom held her gun up, aiming at Miral.

"Stop what you are doing, Miral."

Miral ignored her and kept chanting.

"This is your final warning. STOP or I will fire!"

Miral went quiet and stared directly at mom. Her lips curled into a wicked smile as she held the scepter high in the air. A blazing flash of lightning burst from the clouds and hit the ankh, emitting a blast wave of energy that knocked me back on my butt. Mom didn't budge—she walked forward and emptied her clip firing on Miral.

94

A large "bubble" of energy surrounded the sarcophagus and the priestess. Bullets bounced harmlessly to the side. Mom loaded another clip and kept firing. She was a few feet outside the barrier when she stopped. Miral laughed at her and started chanting again.

I ran to catch up, but my mom held me back from hitting the barrier. I could feel the energy crackling as the hair on my arms started to stand on end.

"I love you, Thomas," my mom whispered, looking on in despair. My dad lay there, seemingly in a coma.

"Mom! We need to do something!"

The ankh glowed brighter and brighter, and a burst of electric energy tendrils blasted into each of the canopic jars. The four jars then sent beams of light at my dad. He started to glow, getting brighter and brighter, until I had to look away.

When the light diminished, I looked back to see my dad standing next to Miral. He took her in his arms and gave her a kiss that could easily be described as more than just friends. The people in thrall behind her began to chant, "Amenhotep, Amenhotep." Both Miral and my dad turned to face them, ignoring us. She held the staff up high again, and another lightning strike powered it.

Slamming the scepter to the ground, Miral began chanting. The energy shield started to grow, and Mom and I had to step back. It grew bigger and bigger, finally encompassing the entire museum. After another strike hit the ankh, she began a new chant. This time, when she banged down, the earth started to shake.

Mom and I were thrown to the ground, as were many of the people who had been taken at the museum. Where the energy bubble had entered the soil, fissures began to form. I couldn't tell what was happening at first, but then I realized that the entire museum was being lifted into the air along with the surrounding grounds. It went up slowly at first, then seemed to gain momentum. Large chunks of soil dropped, along with pieces of connecting underground utilities. Sewer pipes and electrical conduits came crashing down. An old oak tree that had been on the edge fell and plunged to the earth, leaving a large plume of dirt and dust.

Higher and higher it went, finally disappearing into the clouds. My stomach fell and my heart ached. Was my dad gone forever?

"Mom, I need to go home."

"I'm not sure I can leave, Honey. Beyond your dad, I have to organize the police for... for something, I guess."

"Okay. You stay here and let me know what's going on. I'm going to see if there's anything at Dad's store that can help."

She nodded, half in shock. "Talk to Nomi, too. There's a slim chance, but maybe she might have some idea?"

"I will."

I gave her a hug, trying to hold back my tears. "I love you, Mom."

"I love you, too, Honey."

14

My breaths were coming out in short spurts as I plowed through the door to my room, taking the stairs two at a time to get there. Beans was right where I had left him on the bed.

"Zzzz..."

"Beans, can you wake up?"

"Zzzz..."

I picked him up, gently shaking him to try to wake him up.

"Beans?"

It seemed like the psychic strength it took him to warn me before had drained him entirely; he wouldn't budge. I put him back down and tucked him in. Turning around, I ran straight into Daniel.

"Whoa... You okay, Tamzin?"

Even though I should've been surprised to see him, not much could surprise me nowadays. I didn't even think anything of it. "No, I'm not okay."

I quickly told him what had happened up until this point. Just as I was finishing, voice barely audible and shakier than I would have liked, he hugged me tightly. And in that moment, I couldn't be strong anymore. The tears came with a vengeance. He held me, rubbing his hand along my arm to try and soothe me, then gently pushed me away, looking into my eyes.

"What can I do to help?"

"I don't know... I honestly don't know what to do."

"The scarab brooch?"

"Yes! Let's grab it and bring it to Nomi. She might have an idea."

We rushed down the stairs and into the *Dungeon*. I spied the box on the shelf and grabbed for it. For some reason, my hand was knocked away. What the hell? The antique doll was leaning toward the box, its hand in the way. Its face seemed more rotting and decrepit than normal as it sneered at me. Good God, I could *not* deal with this right now.

"Whatever the hell you are, get the hell away from me. Now!"

The doll seemed to fall backward, releasing the box.

"Tamzin, did you say something?" asked Daniel.

"Nope... Let's go!"

"Uhm..." He gave me a funny look, like he knew I had said something, but then his face turned serious again. "Yeah, okay, let's go."

"Sorry, no time to explain." I gave him a sheepish look as we headed out.

We ran out and down the street to Nomi's as quickly as we could manage. Luckily, the door was open. She had a customer in her private seance parlour in the back, and I almost started hyperventilating. I didn't know what to do, so I just stood there, panicking. Daniel walked up to the glass counter and hit the bell.

"Probably not the best time to be polite," he said.

"True."

I hit the bell a few more times, and she appeared, along with the Mayor.

"Yumi?"

"Oh, hello Tamzin. Is everything okay?"

"No. My mom is at the museum. It's gone."

"Gone? What do you mean gone?"

"This is going to sound crazy, but it was taken up into the sky."

She stood still, face emotionless, almost like she was waiting for the punch line. I guess Mom didn't tell her about all the supernatural stuff relating to Jack the Ripper... She probably thought that I was insane right now.

"What?"

"Maybe it's best if you get there and talk with my mom? Seeing is believing."

She seemed to be considering it, then came to a decision. "Okay, I will."

Yumi shook Nomi's hand, giving me and Daniel a worried look as she headed out the door.

"Come in the back and tell me what is happening."

We went through the curtain, entering the seance room. It was crazy with different odds and ends everywhere, but I always felt safe here when I was younger.

"That Mayor Turner is a tough read. Her future path is like mist in a fog," she said as she sat down. "Okay, please tell me what has you so worried."

"It's my dad. He's in trouble."

I quickly explained the circumstances. She nodded and appeared to consider everything I told her, as if she actually believed what I said. Nomi was great.

"May I see the brooch?" Nomi asked.

"Sure, here it is."

I handed her the box, and she proceeded to open it up.

"Ahhh, there you are," she said with recognition.

"Have you seen it before?"

"Yes. I was the one who sent it to you."

"What? Where did you get it?"

"Actually... I won it in a poker game."

"A poker game?"

"Yes, in London. When it came up as a potential payment on a bet, I could feel it calling to me. I realized it was important, so I went for it."

"Wow. I didn't even know you played poker."

"Well... We all have to survive somehow, you know. I actually had to cheat to win, which I would never do under any other circumstance. I knew, though, that it was special."

The fact that Nomi just admitted to cheating at poker made me laugh. It also made me wonder how easy it was for her to cheat...

"Why did you send it to me?"

"After I left with what I had won, I examined it carefully. As I touched it, I sensed you and your dad back home. I didn't know why, but I decided to send it along. I had actually forgotten about it since I sent it a few months ago when I was traveling."

"Well, it's tied to Prince Amenhotep's servant, I guess. When the priestess stabbed and killed her, it must have been linked to her spirit."

"Yes, that would seem to be the case... Let me think for a moment on what we can do to help your father."

She went to her books on the wall and started going through them. I had so much nervous energy building up inside me that I started pacing. After a few minutes, Daniel grabbed my hand.

"Hey, I'm here for you."

He pulled me close, rubbing my shoulders with his firm grip. We both sat at the table. The silence in the room was deafening.

"Here! This may be of help."

She brought the book to the table and thumbed to a certain section.

"It's about astral projection. Or, more specifically, about a chant that can project a spirit from a body."

I looked at Daniel and we both shrugged.

"How do we do it?"

"We are looking to project you, Tamzin, to the museum. We use the scarab brooch as our focal point. We use Daniel's energy as a boost. Maybe, just maybe, it will work."

"Okay, let's do it."

"Hang on," Daniel said, holding up a hand. "Do we know if this will actually work? Are there risks of losing Tamzin in the nether? Will we be able to pull her back into her body?"

"I don't know. I believe she will come back on her own."

"But, if her tether breaks because of all this other magic being released by the priestess, will she be able to find her body? And us?"

"Daniel, you know I have to try," I said. I pleaded with him, searching his eyes and squeezing his hands. He furrowed his brow, shaking his head.

"I don't like this... I don't want to risk losing you."

"Daniel, it's my decision. I'm going." I let go of his hand and turned my body toward Nomi. "Okay, Nomi, let's get this over with."

"I believe in you, Tamzin. You will come back, and I think you will find your dad." Nomi did a sort of bow toward me, then gave me a hug.

Daniel was silent. He stood next to me, jaw clenched. I knew that he was worried, but there was no talking me out of helping my dad.

"Tamzin, you hold onto the scarab. We should all hold hands around my crystal ball. Its energy will also aid us."

We sat positioned as she said. I was nervous, but there was no stopping now.

"Okay, girl, focus on your father. Daniel, you think of her father as well. Concentrate as I begin my chant. And remember, you will be a spirit—you will not be able to interact with items in this state. I don't know what else you will or won't be able to do."

"Will I be able to communicate with my dad?"

"I think so, as long as there is some of his spirit still present. But, this is uncharted territory."

I gave Daniel one last look. His smile was tight, but he nodded, and I knew that meant that he was okay with letting me go, even though he didn't like it. I squeezed his hand tighter and focused.

I thought of my dad in the antique shop. I thought of him making pancakes. I thought of him hugging me. I pictured him in the audience at one of my dance recitals. I heard his voice telling me that he loved me.

Nomi's chanting was quiet, yet strong. I couldn't make out the words but I could feel their power. For a moment, I wondered what it would be like to be Daniel, a tethered spirit. Then, my eyes closed.

All of the air was sucked out of my lungs. My body was buffeted with many sensations, ranging from smells to colors to bumps to whispers and whines. I felt as if I was moving through the air. This lasted for a few moments, then suddenly I was surrounded by blackness and could breathe again.

I couldn't see anything, but I still tried to move. Slam! My knee hit the edge of something, and it stung. There would definitely be a bruise there tomorrow.

Wait... Wasn't I supposed to be a spirit? Did it not work?

"Tamzin."

I jumped back, smacking my thigh this time.

"Daniel? Is that you?"

"Yep. It looks like I was brought here, also. Well, wherever 'here' is."

"Can you see anything?"

"Not yet. I think I'm still adjusting from the projection."

My eyes began to adjust. My hands found the edge of something that felt like it was made of wood. There was a musty smell, and I felt a slight breeze. Looking around, I was finally able to make things out. The hairs on the back of my arms stood on end as I realized there were dozens of red, glowing eyes looking at us.

"Daniel...."

"I know. I see them, too."

"I'm not a spirit."

"What? How do you know?"

"There's a huge bruise forming on my thigh. Don't get me wrong here, but I don't think spirits are supposed to bruise."

"Shit. Stand behind me."

I crept behind him and tried to hide so they couldn't see me. I knew that Daniel could handle whatever was out there, but I was more fragile. As my eyes further adjusted, I noticed an "Exit" sign in the distance.

"Exit. Straight ahead."

"Got it. Let's go, very quietly."

"You get no complaints from me on that one."

I stepped gingerly, trying to be quiet while keeping Daniel between me and the glowing eyes. We had only gone a few steps when a low growl came from a close pair of eyes. My scarab grew hot and began to glow. I was able to make out what was growling—a saber-toothed tiger! I remembered learning that it was a smilodon when it came to the museum—the body had been partially preserved in an ice floe with two woolly mammoths. Half of its face had some decaying skin, and the other half was bone. Even without its eye, both sockets were glowing as if two eyes were present. The tiger's long dagger teeth gleamed in the little bit of available light.

The beast jumped, looking like it was going to pounce on me. Daniel grabbed it midair, spun around, and threw it back into the sea of eyes. There were hoots, whines, and other animal noises as the smilodon smashed into the other creatures. We must have been in the natural history hall of the museum!

We started running for the exit sign, not even trying to be quiet anymore. There was no point now. Halfway there, something grabbed onto my hair and yanked me backward.

"Daniel!"

He turned and grabbed the vulture that was trying to attack me. Partially tangled in my hair, the bird split in half as Daniel pulled. Both sides kept moving, even when its body was literally just ripped in half. Finally, the vulture was still and its eyes went dark as it dropped to the ground.

We sprinted to the door but were stopped short by more creatures. A number of small animals started crawling up my legs, scratching with their claws as they climbed. I grabbed one, then another, tossing them away. Daniel began hurling them, but they kept coming at us. I felt like a pincushion that was being torn apart. We had almost made it to the exit, but the small re-animated corpses were weighing me down.

There was a low rumble which turned into a teeth-chattering roar. After a second of silence following the noise, the rodents started to drop away and flee. When I looked back, most of the glowing eyes had also retreated. I wasn't sure what that sound was, but it had saved us. We threw the doors open, rushed out, and slammed them behind us. I was out of breath and in pain from all of the scratches on my body, but we'd made it.

I turned to look at Daniel to see if he was as relieved as I was when I saw a quick movement out of the corner of my eye. A large set of teeth grabbed Daniel and threw him like a rag doll across the lobby. PAM! I had completely forgotten about her.

I slowly turned and came face to skull with the T-rex. There was light streaming in from the massive skylight, so I was able to see her in her full glory. Her glowing eyes were massive and some of her teeth were the size of my head. It seemed like she was studying me, at least for now. I knew that she could crush me without batting an eyelash. Uhm… not that she had eyelashes.

"Hey, you," Daniel yelled from behind. "Eat this!"

He threw a crowbar at her. As she turned, it cracked into her lower jaw. Taking the opportunity, I bolted toward the front door. Pam looked back my way and started charging forward, slowly at first then quickly picking up speed. She was about to grab me with her teeth when I dove behind the front counter. The T-rex crashed into it, sending shards of glass and plastic flying everywhere. The counter luckily remained intact, keeping me hidden from her for the moment. Daniel sprinted over to me and grabbed my arm, helping me up.

"Tam, you good?" he asked, voice calm and steady.

I, on the other hand, was gasping for air when I said, "Yup, I'm fine. Man, I am not in good enough shape for all of this…" Daniel smiled at me, squeezing my shoulder.

"Course you are. Now let's try to get out of here."

As we were eyeing the main entrance, the reanimated body of bones swung its tail at the doors. One bash from those bones and I'd be done for. I pointed to the stairs and we made a run for them. The T-rex took a moment to figure out what we were doing, so we got there first and started to climb.

I made it to the second floor, Daniel right behind me, when Pam had finally reached us and gave one big snap of her jaws, catching Daniel's arm and tearing off part of his sleeve.

"Woah, that was close," he said, rubbing at his now bare arm.

"Are you okay?"

"Yeah, the skeleton got some sleeve but no Daniel."

The T-rex was pacing the floor, keeping one of its glowing eyes focused on us. We were on the second floor, but the entire middle was open to the lobby with the skylight above. I wasn't sure we could make it to an exit without getting ripped to pieces.

"Thoughts?" Daniel asked.

"Not yet, but I'm thinking."

We looked around for any way to escape or at least some kind of weapon to help us out. Scanning the area, I noticed a massive chandelier hanging over the lobby. Its base was tied to part of the ceiling that wasn't a skylight, directly in the center of the room. Some of the ceiling around it had fallen, probably when the building was uprooted. There were four guide wires linking to points on the walls of the second floor.

"Daniel, do you see the chandelier? It looks like it's loose."

"Yeah, you're right."

"Let's each grab a guide wire and see if we can give it a push to loosen it up more."

"Got it. I'll head onto the other side of this floor."

As Daniel ran, Pam kept looking back and forth between us. Still, though, she seemed to be more focused on me. On the opposite side, he yanked the guide wire from its tether on the wall. My wire took a lot of tugging, but finally, I pulled it away from its sconce.

I tugged and tugged, pulling with all my strength, kind of like a tug of war. My side of the war only moved the massive chandelier about an inch or so. Daniel gave it a yank and it swung his way. Using the return momentum, I pulled harder and managed to get it to swing a little bit closer to me. Once again, Daniel pulled as it went back his way.

We went back and forth like this for a while when finally another chunk of the roof fell to the floor. My arms were tired, and my hope for this plan was quickly diminishing with each swing. I felt something hot in my pocket, and I realized that the scarab was glowing. I pulled it out, trying to figure out what it wanted. Holding it up to get a better view, a bolt of lightning hit the top of the roof, burning through the ceiling like a sharp knife.

The chandelier came crashing down, partially blocking Pam's path to the back entrance.

"Tamzin!" Daniel yelled from across the lobby.

"Let's go!"

I sprinted down the back stairs, meeting Daniel right in front of the doors. I tried the first door, but it was locked. Feverishly, I pushed on the second door—also locked... Pam had made her way around the side and was vaulting toward us. I froze for a moment as her jaws opened in front of me.

Daniel pulled me into the next door, which he had pried open. Just as we were slamming it shut, the re-animated skeleton crashed into the doors. Two of them shattered, scattering glass everywhere, including on the both of us. She shoved her snout through the door as she snapped at us, but the rest of her was too large to get through. Thank the gods.

We were in what used to be the back parking lot. Apparently, a fair bit of land around the museum came with it into the sky. Instead of blacktop with lines to park in, this area had morphed into a huge grassy field. Overhead, the sky was mostly sunny with only a few clouds, which made me realize that we must have been above the roiling storm over the city. Bolts of lightning blasted from the clouds, seeming to strike some kind of lightning rod in the distance. The occasional thunder boom would sound, but otherwise, the only noise was the wind whistling.

We headed toward where the blasts were coming down. Getting closer, the scene resembled a science fiction film. The homeless were surrounding the base of an incomplete pyramid that wasn't much taller than we were. In the middle of the structure was the scepter. The ankh was being hit, and electric tendrils went out to the people on the outside. This energy was then emitted as light toward the base of the pyramid, where the stones were slowly forming and building. The homeless were frozen in place, but they didn't seem to be physically harmed.

We crept past, and no one seemed to notice. Coming to a fork in the path, we saw an opening to what looked like a garden maze on the left, and a road that curved over the horizon on the right. The garden area reminded me of the one from my dream, so we headed that way. Right as we entered the garden area, a voice rang out.

"Stop!"

Quickly glancing over my shoulder, I saw my dad. I ran over and grabbed him to give him a hug.

"Dad! I thought you were going to be sacrificed. We've been looking for you."

As I hugged him, I realized that he felt different. He was stiff and didn't bend over to hug me back.

"Dad?"

I searched his eyes and found no hint of recognition.

"I am the brother of Prince Amenhotep!"

"What?"

"Your father is gone. I now inhabit this flesh."

His smile was twisted in a malevolent way. This guy was definitely not one of the good guys.

"I know you're in there, Dad. Fight him!"

The invader laughed at me.

"He is gone. I have devoured his soul."

I realized that my hand was shaking because I was getting so angry. I pulled back, closing my eyes so I wouldn't have to look at my "father" for what I was about to do, and punched him as hard as I could in the face. My hand bounced off and a shock of pain ran up my entire arm.

"Guards! Take these two away!"

Two security guards showed up and dragged us away. Daniel looked at me, raising a questioning eyebrow as if he was asking, *Should we fight?* But I shook my head *No.* I didn't want to harm my dad, anymore than I may have already with that punch. As far as I was concerned, all of the people under the priestess's thrall were innocent. Daniel could do some real damage if he tried anything.

We were escorted in the other direction from the garden, off over the horizon. The wind whistled louder and louder as we moved forward. There were a set of pillars with chains attached to them. Looking further, I realized that the high-pitched gusting sound was coming from the edge of the landmass where it dropped away. Taking a peek over the ledge, I saw roiling clouds with lightning blasting back and forth. I definitely didn't want to fall off the edge.

We were chained to the pillars, along with a young woman that appeared to be crying.

"Are you okay?" I asked her.

"No. I don't know what is happening!"

"What did you see? Were you here when the museum was taken up into the clouds?"

"The last thing I remember was being at the museum with the kids. We had a full class, and I was waiting outside the restroom. Then, I was here! I was working on some kind of garden when I came to my senses. I don't remember going there or anything in between."

"Are the children okay?"

"I think so. From what I could see, they were working on the garden. Dirty, but still in one piece."

"What made you wake up? Do you know?"

"A man was there. He gave me a kiss and told me he wanted me to be his servant. The next thing I knew a woman came by and told me I was to be punished for seducing the man. Security guards came and chained me here."

"So, you woke up when the woman came?"

"Yes, I think so. I remember the man, but I was still foggy then."

Daniel was fiddling with the shackles.

"I think I can break these," he said.

"Hang on... Someone's coming."

We stopped talking, trying to look as inconspicuous as possible. I suddenly realized what I had been having nightmares about—a full-on mummy came ambling down the path. He was tall and gaunt. Bandages hung down in some spots, and in others, you could see his rotting flesh. His movements were stiff, but I sensed an underlying strength. Similar to the beasts in the natural history wing, his eyes were glowing red.

Daniel stood between the creature and me as it approached. The monster went for the teacher, though. She began to scream as he tore her away from the chain and shackles. One of her hands was left dangling and the other had its skin torn off. It took everything I had not to puke. He carried her to the edge as she kicked and yelled at the top of her lungs. He threw her, and she flew a long way out before she began falling downward. Her screams echoed, then faded off into nothingness.

I stared at the hand left in the shackle, cringing. A tugging on my chains brought me back to reality. Daniel was holding the shackle between his hands. He was straining with the effort, then it snapped. He did the same with my other hand when the mummy grabbed me.

A current of electricity went between us when the mummy touched me. He stood still, and his eyes stopped glowing for a moment. I had a weird feeling in my stomach, but I didn't know what was happening. I was about to reach up to his face when the glowing started again. Looking directly into my eyes, he froze, let me go, then started ambling back up the trail.

Daniel snapped his chains and ran to go after him.

"Wait. Daniel, wait."

"Why? He just killed that woman!"

"I don't know. I'm not sure what just happened, but I think I felt a connection to him."

Daniel furrowed his brow, then shrugged. "You better not be wrong about this..."

We crept back up the path, coming to the edge of the garden maze. We sat down, hidden behind a tree, to take a second to rest from everything that had just happened. I was jittery because I knew that we didn't have much time, but if I didn't rest now, I didn't know how much longer I'd be able to keep it together.

I crossed my legs out in front of me, resting my head on Daniel's shoulder. I clasped my hands together in my lap, and when I looked down, I was visibly shaking. Daniel seemed to notice and put his hand over mine to try to steady my tremors.

"Hey," he said, rubbing his thumb over my fingers. "We're going to make it through this."

I sighed, closing my eyes and taking a moment to enjoy the silence before answering him. "Yeah, well, easier said than done."

He chuckled to himself. "I guess it seems like right when things appear to be going well, everything turns to shit."

"You can say that again. I don't even know what I'm doing anymore, honestly. Things were just so much easier before..."

"Before you met me?" Daniel asked, body tensing.

I cringed. "Oh my God, that is *not* what I meant. Don't even say that. I can't picture life without you. Who else would keep me company when I didn't want to be alone?" I was trying to lighten the mood, but he wasn't having it.

"Jimmy?" Daniel asked, voice laced with what I could only describe as jealousy.

I was taken aback by his blunt response. Daniel never seemed to get jealous, so I wasn't sure what had changed. And we never really talked about Jimmy.

"I mean, c'mon, Tamzin. You know however much I do for you, however much you mean to me, that at the end of the day you're still with him. Not me. I know things are complicated," he said, voice rising a little as he let go of my hand and ran his fingers through his hair, "but I never asked for any of this!" He stood up and began pacing in front of me. "I never asked to die, to be *murdered*. I never asked to find a beautiful girl that I could just so happen to interact with even though no one else noticed me before. I never asked to fall for you. Being with you is all I ever think about, all I ever *want*, but it's torture because I know that you can never truly be mine. I'm not even *alive*, for God's sake. What kind of life would that be for you?"

"Daniel, please," I said, trying to keep my voice steady. Tears were blurring my vision, and I swiped them away.

"When I saw that mummy take that woman and throw her over the edge, I could only think about you the whole time. How I was *glad* that it was her and not you that he took." He put his head in his hands, letting out a low, irritated moan. "I'm such a terrible person."

It felt like my heart was breaking. I never knew that he felt this way, so trapped by himself and, worse, by me. I stood up, grabbing Daniel's hand.

"I... I don't even know what to say, Daniel. There's nothing wrong with wanting to protect me. You know I would feel the same way if I thought the mummy could have done something to you. If you think that's what it means to be a terrible person, to actually *care*, then I would like to know what you believe a good person would be thinking in that situation."

I paused, wanting to continue but not knowing how to put my feelings into words. "Daniel, I don't want to be something that you think you can never have, not based off of how I feel about you anyway. Do you honestly believe that?"

He looked down at our entwined hands. "I guess I just didn't want to get my hopes up."

"For the record, it's not like Jimmy and I have a picture perfect relationship. I've been so confused lately, and I know I haven't really been fair to him." I wasn't about to tell Daniel that *he* was the reason why I've been having second thoughts... "You know how the band was trying to find a new lead singer? Well, the other day, Jimmy and said new lead singer kissed. On stage, at a performance. I was literally right in the front, watching the whole thing unfold. He made me feel so stupid, even if she was the one who initiated it. It still hurt me."

Daniel's expression went hard. "How could he do that to you?" he asked, practically shouting. My eyes widened, and I looked around to make sure no one was in our general area to overhear us. "What kind of fool would kiss another girl when he was lucky enough to have you? I hope you know that he's not worthy of you, especially not if he would do something like that. I would never do something so stupid." He pulled me in for a hug, stroking my hair. "I'm sorry," he whispered, cradling my head.

I smiled, but it was a sad smile. Why couldn't all of this just be easy?

15

We headed into the walled shrub area. There was a small pond, and the children from Saint Stephen's Academy were doing gardening chores. At first, we were trying to be stealthy, just in case one of the kids tried something. But after a few minutes of looking around, we realized that the children were ignoring us. It looked like they were planting poppies, and some were blooming way faster than they should have been. There was a trellis over a park bench filled with grapes. Two of the children were picking them and putting them into a basket.

A woman, possibly a teacher, was picking some lotus flowers and arranging them on a towel.

"Let's see if we can break her trance," I said to Daniel.

"Okay. Careful, though."

I nodded and we approached her.

"Miss, can you help us?" I asked.

No response.

"Miss, are you a teacher with Saint Stephen's?"

No response.

Maybe human contact would break her free? I reached over and gently touched her shoulder. She stood up and turned around, looking directly at me. She opened her mouth and hissed, pointing at me. I backed away as she came at me. Daniel grabbed my arm and we tried to get further away from her.

The students seemed to notice. One by one, they copied her hissing and pointed directly at me. Stalking towards us, we were backed up against the shrub wall. We probably could have fought our way out, but I didn't want to hurt anyone. They were innocent pawns in all of this.

The sound of laughter came from the entrance. Miral! And my dad was with her. As they came over, the students parted to make way. Miral stood right before me, looking me up and down.

"Well, young Tamzin, how did you get up here?"

She looked at Daniel, furrowed her brow, then smiled.

"Maybe it was this boyfriend of yours? He does seem quite… *different*, if I do say so myself." She scraped her finger up his chest, tapping him on the nose.

"I want my father back," I demanded, looking her directly in the eye.

"Well, that cannot happen. His soul was absorbed when my lover took him."

I wanted to attack her, moving toward her to do some kind of damage, but Daniel held me back.

"Your father would be happy to be with me, though. He loved Miral, and she loved him."

"Give him back to me!"

She seemed to tire of talking and turned away.

"Follow me. Follow me or I will throw all of these young student friends of yours off the edge as I did with their teacher."

I looked at Daniel and we both sighed. I was losing hope, but I realized that I had to save my dad. We followed them.

~

We were heading up the trail to the pyramid-in-process. It now had an arched entryway, with an ankh symbol prominently displayed. The hall entrance was like a tunnel, and torches lined the way—they were in sconces embedded into the walls. I guess the magical process of forming the pyramid even included all of these elaborate details. We got to the end of the hall, and it opened into a large room.

And let me just say, the magic was *definitely* elaborate. There were tapestries on the walls. Wall sculptures were inset with busts of pharaohs and various gods. Frescoes of the priestess and the prince's younger brother acted as a backdrop to a large throne with two massive chairs. There was a second floor in the process of being built with stairs on both sides of the room. It had modern banisters, with pillars supporting the balconies that overlooked the throne room.

Between the chairs was the ankh scepter. It reached up toward the open roof and was struck by a lightning bolt, sending out tendrils of energy to the homeless slaves outside to keep the building process in motion. This happened a few times each minute.

"This is my seat of power," Hatshepsut said as she folded her arms. "I rule this land. I rule you!"

She was looking directly at me.

"Please let my father go. He's innocent."

"Your father pleased my host. He also pleases me." She smiled a wicked smile, tilting her head to the side.

"What do you hope to accomplish, up here in the sky?" I asked.

She contemplated my question for a moment.

"This is only my seat of power. Once we have rebuilt my home, we are going to conquer the lands below. Only world domination shall sate me. All will bow before me!"

Wow, she had quite the god complex. I guess she did manage to come back from the dead... I wasn't sure what else to say.

"Boy, come here," she said, pointing to Daniel.

I shrugged my shoulders at him and he stepped forward. She grabbed his chin and inspected him more closely than before.

"Undead... You bring me a gift, Tamzin!"

She raised her hand and another blast hit the ankh. This time, the energy tendril went to her hand, and she slammed it into Daniel's chest. He stumbled back, falling to the ground.

"Daniel!" I ran over and grabbed him, trying to shield him from Miral. I pulled on his shoulder to help him get up. When he looked at me, I started shaking—his eyes were glowing red.

"No! Daniel!"

He stood up and walked over to Miral, taking up a guarding stance behind her.

"And now, your friend is mine. You can do nothing. You *are* nothing!"

I couldn't take this anymore. I ran up to her seething with anger, literally ready to kill, but Daniel and my dad grabbed my arms and held me back.

I tried to shake out of their grip, but they were too strong. "Let me go!"

"Chain her. Let her gaze upon my glory as I become a god!"

They dragged me to a pillar at the corner of the room, shackling my arms to its chains.

"Dad. Dad, please. Don't do this."

"I am not your father."

"I know you're in there, Dad. Please help me."

The man, my father, looked at me with cold disdain. "Your father is gone."

And with that, they left me. I watched them walk back to their priestess. I felt alone—alone and defeated. I dropped to my knees, tears dampening my cheeks. I had nobody on my side. Daniel was hers, and I was utterly alone.

~

I cried for a while, probably longer than I should have, then decided not to feel sorry for myself anymore. What could I do to get out of this situation? I was chained to a pillar, which was maybe a head taller than me. My hands were shackled, but my feet were free. I had freedom of motion all the way around and could move a few steps away.

Everyone had left the throne room. The only sign of life was an occasional slave worker that was going in and out, but I wasn't really sure what she was actually doing.

Looking at what I had available, there was a large vase that held a plant next to one wall. It was just out of reach, and I don't know what I could do with it even if I was able to get my hands on it. There was a chaise lounge nearby. On the back wall was a huge tapestry depicting Miral and my dad, with a huge glowing ankh between them.

I sunk down to the ground, feeling defeated. There was no way I could get out of here. I shifted my position to get more comfortable to wallow in self-pity when, all of a sudden, I felt a sharp pain coming from my pocket area. Something had stabbed me—the scarab brooch! I had completely forgotten about it. The

115

chains allowed me enough freedom to move a little, so I pulled it out and extended the pin. It was creepy, especially since I dreamed about it being used to stab me in the heart, but it restored some of my hope. After all, the pin was sort of why I was here in the first place.

The shackles seemed old, so the lock shouldn't be too hard to pick. When I was younger, I went through a phase where I picked plenty of locks. My dad had a bunch of old safes and handcuffs, and I spent many afternoons playing with them. I was getting pretty good at it too… until I met Jimmy. Then, everything changed.

Speaking of Jimmy, I wondered what he was doing. Was he aware of what was happening at the museum? Did he know I was here? Did he even care? Okay, maybe that was a little harsh, but he hurt me. We never even got to talk about the whole kiss thing. We haven't really gotten to talk about much of anything lately. I've been telling myself that we're both busy, but I don't know if I can lie to myself anymore. Things just haven't been working, and I've been avoiding him. I haven't even *wanted* to see him. I love him, and I know that I always will, but I'm starting to feel… restless? All of the little things that I used to love about Jimmy have just been annoying me lately. The fact that he hadn't even crossed my mind until right now… well, I think that just about says it all.

Daniel and I have already been through so much in such a short period of time. He was always there for me and made me feel better just by being with me. Jimmy didn't make me feel like Daniel did. I haven't been feeling any sparks with him lately—I'm not the same person I was three years ago when we started dating. I've changed so much just recently, so it only makes sense for this to happen. But it's still hard for me to wrap my brain around the fact that the only guy I've ever been with might not be "the one".

Okay, Tamzin, stop thinking. You need to get this done…

I hid behind the pillar and began to work my magic, the entire process coming back to me quickly, as if it were just yesterday that I had been doing this with my dad. I slipped the tip of the pin into the keyhole and started fiddling. It was an old-fashioned mechanism, so I was able to feel through the interior mechanics pretty easily. I gave the end of the pin a slight bend, using leverage against the exterior of the lock. Reinserting the pin, I did some more fiddling, another adjustment, more fiddling, and *click*! The shackle fell to the ground. The second one was much quicker. Before I knew it, I was free and clear—well, free of the shackles anyway. I decided to check one of the corridors that connected to the larger chamber.

This hallway was similar to the main entrance with torches on the wall, but it dead ended into stone. There were two thresholds along the wall, one on each side. I tiptoed toward the closest one, to my right. I heard someone in the distance, so I ran into the entrance and hugged the wall, trying not to breathe, which was proving to be much more difficult than they make it look in the movies. A security guard walked past me, heading toward the main chamber.

The hall opened into a room with some artifacts. Everything was arranged very carefully, almost as if they had been part of a ceremony. The center of the room held a sarcophagus and pedestals with canopic jars surrounding it. This was close to the setup that the priestess used on my father. Up close and personal, the sarcophagus and jars were bigger than I thought. I picked up the one with a falcon head. Heavier than I would have thought, too. I was looking at the detail when...

"Put that down!"

I looked up to see my dad, brow furrowed, looking angrier than I've ever seen him. I stared at him, chin held high, gaze steady, and said, "No."

He slowly came closer, and I backed up. I tripped on the corner of the coffin but regained my balance, straightening up. The color drained from his face, and he almost looked afraid. Hmmm...

"Let my dad go."

"Your father is gone. I have no control over that fact."

I held the pottery above my head. He practically jumped up.

"Please, put the jar down."

My decision was made.

"This is for my dad," I said as I smashed the canopic jar to the ground. Pottery fragments shattered across the floor, and the interior contents turned to dust. The younger prince fell to his knees.

"And this is for Daniel."

I grabbed the next jar and threw it against the wall. It exploded, its contents evaporating into the air.

"Stop. Please stop..." He was gasping for air. I wanted payback, especially after feeling so powerless this entire time.

"Give me my dad back!"

"I am sorry. I am unable to do that."

The final two jars crashed on top of the sarcophagus. Nothing had felt more satisfying than that.

He stopped moving. I eyed him, making sure he wasn't going to try anything, then went to him. He wasn't breathing... I didn't really know how to do CPR, but I've seen people do it on TV before and I needed to try something. I did compressions on his chest.

"Come on, Dad."

I kept trying, but I didn't get a heartbeat.

"Dad, you can't leave me!"

At this point, I was practically pounding on his chest out of sheer desperation. Tears were blurring my vision and my voice was getting shaky.

"Dad, I can't lose you. Not now, not like this. What am I going to do without you?" I managed to get all the words out between choking breaths. I stopped pounding on his chest, falling back on my knees. His eyes were wide open, blankly staring at the ceiling.

He was gone...

I stood up, pinching the remaining tears out of my eyes. I couldn't cry anymore—I was all out of tears. I wanted to hit someone or smash something or torture the monster that overtook my dad's body. I had never felt so useless in my life. I wanted to scream.

I took another look at my dad, seeing his lifeless eyes stare off into nothing. I knelt down beside him, carefully lifting my hand to close his eyes. The beetle felt warm in my pocket, but I didn't really think anything of it at the time. I gently put my fingers over his eyelids, smoothing them down. When our skin touched, I felt a zap of electricity.

Suddenly, he gasped air.

I jumped. "Dad? Is that you?"

I had no idea if it was actually him, but I cradled his head in my arms.

"Please be my dad," I whispered.

"You making pancakes?"

I wanted to punch him, but a burst of other emotions rushed through me. Mostly, I felt a massive relief. Dad was alive!

"Dad, we need to figure out a way out of here."

"Where is here?"

"Uhm... let me explain."

I went through the story with him. He was dumbfounded, but he still believed me. We took a minute to rest and regain our strength before heading out.

16

I gave my dad a hug as we ventured out into the corridor.

"I'm going to try to get the scepter, Dad. You keep Miral occupied."

"I'm not sure if I can fool her, but I'll try."

"Just use your suave seduction skills. She will never know what hit her." I tried to keep a straight face as I said that, but I couldn't do it. We both burst out laughing.

We had to calm our breathing as we quietly entered the throne room. We both stepped into a shaded area, watching Miral. The priestess opened a small trunk, revealing jewels and gold dinnerware. She took out all of the pieces, one by one, and examined them as she ran her hand over their surfaces. She placed the treasures on a stone table, setting them out in some kind of order. Dad gave me a look, nodded his head, then sauntered over to her. I remained hidden in the shadows.

"Hello, my love," she said, partially distracted.

Dad cleared his throat. "What are you doing, my dear?"

"This chest holds many of our original personal items. I am checking for damage."

I hugged the wall, leaving my area of shade, creeping in the opposite direction of the priestess. I went past the chain pillar I had been tied to earlier, then snuck by the hallway leading outside. I worked my way around the other wall and passed the stairs to the second floor. Lightning struck the ankh, and I jumped.

"I've decided that we shall have a great banquet tonight. All of our slaves shall come and watch as their gods feast. Does that appeal to you, my highness?"

"Yes. That sounds divine."

"We can use some of our gold finery. It will be like old times."

I continued to make my way along the wall. I finally made it to the throne, and the priestess had her back to me. I bounded forward, ducking down behind the chair. The ankh beamed with light. Hopefully, I could shut the light down.

I peeked around the corner to see how my dad was doing. Miral finished pulling out the last piece from the trunk.

"Come view some of our old things. It will remind you of our true glory."

My dad looked hesitant to move closer to her, but he went anyway. Looking down at the items, he slid his arm behind the priestess's back.

"Do you remember, my love, where we first kissed?" she asked.

My dad didn't even flinch.

"I do. Do you remember, my love?"

"Yes. It was in the wine room amidst the casks. The smell of grapes was in the air." She looked up at my dad. "Kiss me again."

I froze. I don't know if my dad would be able to pull this off.

He pulled Miral close and gently touched his fingers to her lips. Putting his arms around her, he softly moved in, his lips caressing hers. Miral responded by sinking her body into his, vigorously kissing him back.

Uhm, okay... Maybe my dad could pull it off? For a second, I was angry. How could he do this to Mom? But I guess in this case it was kiss or be killed... He didn't really have much of a choice, but it did seem like he was enjoying it a little too much.

My dad finally pulled away. I don't know if he was channeling his old self or just pretending, but I could see the rapture in his eyes. The priestess stepped away from him.

"You are not my love! What happened? What did you do to him?"

She looked to the pillar where I had been chained. She stamped her foot and pushed my father away.

"Where is the girl? Tamzin! You will pay for what you have done."

Dad backed away as she continued to yell.

"Amenhotep! Subdue this imposter!"

The mummy emerged from one of the corridors behind the throne and stalked toward Dad. Miral ran down the hall where I had rescued my father. The mummy grabbed my dad's arms and held him in place.

"Tamzin, run!"

"I'm not going to leave you, Dad."

I reached for the scepter, but it was too high up for me to grab hold. I ran around to the front of the chairs and climbed. Reaching up, I could almost put a finger on it when another lightning bolt hit. The electric blast from the ankh hit me, and I was thrown to the ground. My hand burned, and my vision was blurry.

"Tamzin! Are you okay?"

"Urgh... Yeah." My head was spinning, but I tried to stand up. Miral stormed back into the room.

"What did you do to the canopic jars?" Her face was beet red, and I thought she might have a stroke.

"Smashed them. Trashed them. Slammed them. I bet the dust from the entrails is still in the air."

"You have killed my love! I will kill your father. Amenhotep, kill him!"

The mummy let go of my father and grabbed him by the neck with his right arm. He began to lift him into the air as my dad struggled to break free. His legs were kicking, and I could only hear choking noises coming from him.

"Stop. Miral, please stop!"

"Miral is dead. And now, your father is dead, too."

The mummy held him up even higher. I ran over, only to be swatted away. I got up and ran in close again, holding onto the mummy's left arm as he tried to shoo me away.

"Please don't kill my dad."

I looked up at the mummy, but he didn't seem to acknowledge me.

"Prince Amenhotep, please don't kill my father."

I felt a slight static shock hit me where I was holding onto the mummy's arm. His body loosened up ever so slightly. I reached up to his rotting head, stroking his cheek.

"Please, Prince Amenhotep. Don't let the priestess control you. I saw you in my dreams—you were a good man."

Suddenly, there was a much stronger zap from his cheek to my finger. Not moving from his side, I left my body.

I was back in Egypt. This time, I was not tied to someone else's point of view. I heard a scream and ran toward the sound. The priestess had plunged the scarab pin into the heart of the servant girl. Finally getting a good look at her, I realized that she was beautiful. She fell back onto the bed, blood stain growing on her linen tunic. She was still, no rise and fall to her chest. I knew that she was dead.

I heard footsteps from the hall, then Prince Amenhotep appeared. He stood in the doorway, looking from his brother to the priestess to the servant girl. He strode in, picking the girl up off the bed. He looked at her, carefully stroking her hair with a shaky hand.

"Husband, let me explain."

He gave the priestess a cold look, not responding.

She looked shocked. "Please, my Amenhotep—"

"Say nothing!" he said, angry voice cutting through the silence that had overtaken the room.

"Brother, the servant girl attacked your wife."

"I said say NOTHING! Leave me... both of you."

The two hung their heads and left the chamber without a word. The prince carried the girl and carefully put her down, gently resting her head on the pillow.

"I am very sorry, Raia."

He ran his thumb over her cheek, sitting down next to her.

"You tried to warn me, but I did not listen. Now, you have paid the ultimate price. And for that, I am truly sorry. I cannot picture a world without you in it."

I moved into the room, looking more closely at the prince. I realized tears were staining his cheeks. He held her hand, bringing it to his lips, and placed a soft kiss in the center of her palm.

"You were always foremost in my heart. I remember the days when we played as children. I could never hide from you—you always found me. When we were together, I felt whole. I have always loved you."

My heart seemed to skip a beat. Maybe from Raia's spirit?

"I should have never married the priestess. You did not believe her to be worthy, and you were correct."

He got up, then knelt down at her side.

"I will avenge you, Raia. They will pay!"

He stood and stalked out of the room.

The mummy looked at me, putting his hand on my cheek. The red glow left his eyes as he slowly lowered Dad to the ground. He turned to me and almost seemed to smile. My heart hurt because he was trapped in this rotting flesh, but I was happy to be with him. Er, Raia was happy. I don't know—I was getting confused between my dream self and reality.

My dad gasped a few breaths, then hugged me. He looked up at the mummy, a mixture of fear and awe crossing his face.

"It's okay, Dad. He's with us now."

"How?"

"Remember when I told you about the dreams I was having of being in old Egypt? The mummy is Prince Amenhotep."

"Wow... the son of the great pharaoh? I wish we could talk with him."

"Uhm... yeah. Let's figure out what to do here, first."

"Yes, yes, sorry. I am always so curious."

We paused for a moment, realizing that the mummy was looking toward the center of the room. Turning around, I could see the look of frustration and anger coming from the high priestess.

"How? How did you do this? He was mine to control!"

"Sorry, lady. You tried to hurt my family—I'm not going down without a fight."

She pointed at the mummy.

"Kill him!"

For a second I didn't realize who she was ordering, but then I saw Daniel charge at the prince. He hit him dead center, both flying back over one of the stone tables. There was dust in the air, so I couldn't really see what was happening. Daniel suddenly flew through the dust, soaring over our heads and smashing into the throne. I knew that he was basically indestructible, but I still winced when his body slammed into the stone.

Prince Amenhotep emerged from the dust and raised an arm toward Daniel. A swarm of flies swirled around Daniel's body. They started to fly into him, pushing him back as he shielded his face from their assault. For some reason, my brain finally put two and two together and realized that the mummy had magical powers. They seemed to coincide with the plagues of Egypt: frogs, boils, and flies. I remembered disease and darkness being part of the story, but I couldn't remember much else.

Daniel was still being pushed back. A bolt of lightning hit the ankh, and the high priestess motioned with her hands. The electric tendril hit the flies, burning them into ash. A plume of smoke went up, and the room smelled like burnt leaves.

Daniel came running and once again tackled the prince, slamming him into the wall. Daniel was pummeling the mummy in the chest and face. My dad grabbed one of the vases and cracked it over Daniel's head. Daniel staggered for a moment, which was enough time for the prince to grab his shoulders and push him back. Step by step, he walked him into the throne. The mummy had his hand on Daniel's throat, locking it against the stone. He reached down and grabbed Daniel's leg, hoisting him over his head.

Daniel's body was thrown up onto the second floor balcony, hitting one of the support pillars with a sickening thud. The pillar cracked but didn't fall down. Daniel slowly got up, shook his head, and leapt over the banister. He landed right on the mummy, knocking him to the ground. Once again, his fists were pounding into the rotting flesh. If he had been a regular mummy without magic, he would have been dust by now.

I noticed a piece of stone that had been broken off one of the tables during the fight. Its edge was sharp and came to a jagged point at the end. I slowly moved toward it, keeping a wary eye on the high priestess. She almost seemed to be enjoying the supernatural battle. I reached down and grabbed the makeshift dagger. Dad saw me and tried to stand between me and Miral so she wouldn't see what I was doing. Now I was determined to make my way over to her.

"Dad, let's try to get to Miral," I whispered.

"Okay. Be careful, though."

I nodded, and we moved along the wall.

The prince kicked Daniel away with one of his legs. He raised his hand and focused on his target. A black mist engulfed Daniel, then started filling up the chamber. It was thicker than a heavy fog and didn't let light through. It was pitch black. I couldn't see anything, but I continued hugging the wall, feeling my way. My dad grabbed my other hand as he followed.

The darkness was so dense that my skin could feel it. It was like a combination of wind and heavy mist. You could feel it swirl around if you moved your hand quickly, but you couldn't see anything. It was not only unnerving, but also disorienting.

A crackle of lightning struck again, eliminating the mummy magic. The black fog evaporated within seconds. Prince Amenhotep was standing over Daniel with a large stone block and brought it smashing down. Daniel, now that the darkness was gone, was able to dodge the slab by rolling to the side. They both proceeded to come together in a clash of rotting flesh and bandages and ghostly resilience.

Crashing and smashing through the room, they destroyed tables, chaise lounges, tapestries, and nearly ran into me and Dad. Prince Amenhotep finally got ahold of Daniel's leg and spun him around, sending him careening toward a wall. He slammed into the wall head first and seemed stunned. The mummy took advantage of the moment and used another one of his Egyptian plagues. A blinding bolt of light hurled toward Daniel, knocking him into the wall again. A cold blast of hail stones started pummeling him. The mummy kept them focused on him and approached the throne.

As the hail kept hitting Daniel, he was soon covered in a layer of ice. The ice got thicker and thicker until you couldn't make him out underneath. The prince slumped onto the throne, and Dad and I ran at the high priestess.

"Don't move!" I said, pointing my stone dagger at her throat.

"You will not win, Tamzin. You cannot win."

My dad whispered, "Have the prince get the ankh. Maybe he can destroy it."

Hatshepsut jumped when he said that, but I held the dagger closer to her.

"My prince, can you get the ankh? It is what powers the priestess."

The mummy looked up at the scepter. He grabbed it with both hands, snapping the wood at the bottom of the scepter in his tight grip. He brought the ankh close, examining it.

"Prince Amenhotep, can you destroy the ankh?"

He almost seemed to nod as he started to crush the totem. After a few moments, he looked at it and it was still in one piece. He put the ankh down on the throne seat and picked up a stone table, smashing it down. The totem was left entirely unscathed. He tilted his head, confused.

Finally, the mummy focused his magical energies on it. Flies, frogs, hail—each one had little to no effect. At this point, I had no idea what to do.

"Dad, any ideas?"

"No, Honey."

"Miral. How do you destroy the ankh?"

She hissed at me. "I do not answer to you, girl."

I held the dagger closer to her neck. She took a ragged breath, then began to laugh. "It cannot be destroyed. It is eternal, like me."

"You're bluffing. You and the prince's brother both told me my dad was gone—but I got him back. Nothing is impossible."

The prince took the ankh in his hands, once again focusing and trying to crush it. A lightning bolt from the clouds came down and hit the totem. The mummy staggered but didn't fall over. I heard a crash—Daniel had broken out of the ice.

Daniel ran to the mummy, realizing that the prince had the ankh. He wound up with both of his hands and hit one of the mummy's arms, hard. A crack sounded and I realized that he had broken the mummy's arm.

"Daniel," I breathed. "Please stop!"

"Destroy the prince," Hatshepsut said.

Daniel wound back his arms again, hitting Prince Amenhotep's thigh like a battering ram. Another crack sounded, and the mummy went down on one knee. He still held onto the ankh, but he was losing the battle.

Daniel put his arms around his adversary's chest. He began to squeeze tighter and tighter. I could almost feel the prince's pain.

"Daniel!"

I was watching the guy I currently liked take out the guy I liked in my dream. Even though I had only touched Raia's spirit, it still felt as if she were part of me. I ran over to my two guys, trying to get between them.

"Daniel, stop. I know you're in there."

"The high priestess has ordered me to destroy him. I must obey."

His eyes glowed red, and I soon realized that there was no arguing with him. He gripped my shoulder tightly, trying to move me out of the way. I cringed, trying not to let the pain get to me. He gripped tighter, and I let out a little yelp.

"Daniel, please. You're hurting me." The mummy seemed to get upset by the fact that Daniel had put me in pain because he stirred, putting his hand over Daniel's on my shoulder. He peeled Daniel's fingers off slowly, one by one, as if he wanted to break each finger. When my shoulder was free from Daniel's grip, I unclenched my fists, which I hadn't realized were clenched, and relaxed my shoulder. I was worried about both of them, and I didn't want to see either get hurt. I don't know why I did it, but I put my arms around both Daniel and the mummy and hugged them.

"I love you, Daniel," I whispered.

I hugged them tighter, not sure what else to do. His arms seemed to loosen up.

"I love you, too, Tamzin."

I paused, shocked. It was Daniel, my Daniel, and he was smiling at me without the crazy red eyes. The spell was broken!

"Now, let's destroy this ankh."

We backed away from the mummy. He was broken and in pain, but he continued to try to crush the totem. Daniel put his hands around it as well. Both of them put their physical and supernatural energy into destroying it. Daniel's face was turning red, and he began to shake.

I was about to suggest trying something else when a tiny explosion shook the building and the ankh shattered into tiny pieces with a blue electric blast wave emanating outward. I was thrown backward, landing on my butt. Standing back up, I noticed that Miral was on the ground, holding her head. My dad was moving toward her to help her to her feet.

"Are you okay, Miral?"

"What happened? I have such a headache," she said, moaning.

"It's okay. We're all okay now."

"Where are we? This doesn't look like the *Mummy Extravaganza*!"

Prince Amenhotep stood up, healed from the fight.

"Oh my God!" Miral said, eyes going wide.

"It's okay, Miral. We have a lot of explaining to do…" I said.

Daniel came over and hugged me.

"I'm sorry. I couldn't stop. She had total control." He motioned toward my shoulder and lifted my sleeve. A small bruise was already forming from where he gripped me. "I can't… I can't believe I did that. I would never touch you like that, to hurt you in any way. I was—"

"Daniel, it's okay. I'll be fine. I know you weren't yourself."

He looked down at his hands as if he were disgusted with himself.

"That doesn't change anything, Tamzin." He held up his hands, palms facing me. "These hands did that to you. And because of that, I will never forgive myself." He hung his head as if he were too ashamed to even look at me.

I lifted his chin up so I could look him in the eye. "Hey, look at me. We made it through this. We did it. And I have you back now. That's all that matters."

My eyes darted from his eyes to his lips, then back to his eyes. He had a sort of longing expression as if he was staring at something that he desperately wanted but could never have. As if he couldn't trust himself around me anymore. That idea broke my heart. In that moment, I wanted nothing more than for him to kiss me. I moved my face closer, my lips just barely brushing his, and whispered, "Daniel, *please*."

He searched my eyes, still looking unsure of himself, but then he cradled my face in his hands and put his lips on mine. I couldn't help but smile against his lips. I wrapped my arms around his neck, deepening the kiss. I didn't want this moment to end. Everything else faded away and it was just me and Daniel, Daniel and me. He held me lightly as if he was afraid that I was going to break.

Slowly, he pulled away. I felt a little light-headed, but it was exhilarating.

"Hold on..." Daniel said playfully. "Did you say that you loved me?"

I eyed him, raising my eyebrows. "Who... me?"

"Yes, you. I heard you say it."

"Hmmm..."

"Well, I love you. I'm not afraid to throw that out there," he said, standing up straight.

I paused, thinking about it for a second. The more I thought about it, the more I realized it was true. "I love you, too," I said.

He kissed me again and suddenly, it felt like gravity had just turned off—I was falling. It was like a rollercoaster ride and my cart had just started descending down the highest drop. My stomach felt like it was going into my throat, and my hair lifted of its own accord. *What the hell?*

We were all looking around, confused, when we realized what was happening. The museum was falling back to earth!

17

"What do we do?" I looked desperately at my dad.

"I don't know." He was still holding Miral up.

A group of the school students came rushing in. They looked around, unsure of what was happening. Some of them gathered around me, asking a flurry of questions.

"Are we falling?"

"What's happening?"

"How did we get here?"

Their little faces looked up at me with worry, and some of them were crying. I knelt down to their level, and lied through my teeth.

"It's going to be okay. Just stay together. Hold hands, okay?"

They nodded and formed into a group. At least they wouldn't die alone.

My pocket felt warm—I realized that I still had the scarab brooch. I pulled it out, and the heat radiated, but I had no idea what to do with it. How could it help a falling mass of land?

The room suddenly grew dark. The kids gasped and the crying became worse. Looking up through the open roof, I realized that we had entered the storm clouds. Bolts of lightning and ear piercing thunder rang out, but they were no longer focused on us. The chamber got lighter, and I realized that we were below the main clouds.

I wanted to say something to my dad because, at this point, it seemed like we were doomed, but there had to be something I could do. Think, Tamzin, think! I held the scarab and it started glowing.

Raia, I heard. Where was that voice coming from? The scarab? *Raia, come to me.*

For some reason, I knew the voice. It was Prince Amenhotep. I looked over at the mummy. He was crumpled and laying against the throne. Daniel stood next to him, and I ran over.

"He collapsed when we destroyed the ankh."

"He's talking to me... In my head."

"Like Beans?"

"Yeah."

Daniel picked him up and sat him on the throne. I jumped up next to him, putting my hand in his. I took the scarab and touched it to his chest. The brooch grew hotter and the light was getting stronger. The mummy gently gripped my hand.

Prince Amenhotep was running down a hall. His brother and the high priestess ducked into a room. The prince reached the doorway, his large frame blocking the entire door.

"Why did you kill Raia? She has been my servant, my friend, since I was a small child."

"It wasn't us, brother. We walked in and she had already been stabbed."

"I know you both conspired. I know what you have been doing behind my back. Raia, though, had no sin. By killing her you have killed yourselves!"

"Brother, we had nothing to do with it. There must have been some other conspirators who took her life."

The prince walked forward and grabbed his brother. He threw him against the wall. Moving forward to grab him, he started banging his head into the stone. The high priestess pulled out her ceremonial ankh totem. She moved a lever on the front and a blade came out of the bottom. She walked up to the prince and stabbed him deep in his shoulder, then tugged the blade back out.

Prince Amenhotep turned around and slapped her. She landed on the bed. Amenhotep threw his brother through the door and into the hall, following after him.

The brother spied a sword hanging on the wall and pulled it down. He was brandishing it as the prince came out. He lunged forward, but the older brother sidestepped. He grabbed the companion sword off the wall and they began to fight.

Down the hall, they thrust and parried, knocking over vases and cutting up tapestries. The clatter of the swords echoed throughout the palace. The battle moved back into the room outside of the

132

prince's bed chambers. The brother was outmatched, but Prince Amenhotep had the stab wound and was losing blood.

The prince glanced into the bedroom and saw Raia's lifeless body on the bed. He paused for only a moment, but his brother thrust his sword, piercing the prince through his abdomen and out the other side.

With her dead eyes looking back at him, Prince Amenhotep's rage grew. The sword was embedded in him but he kept slashing at his brother, who backed out onto the balcony. Amenhotep plunged his blade into the traitor's heart.

"You are avenged, Raia."

Blood spurted from the younger man's mouth. He reached up and grabbed onto the prince's tunic.

"I take you with me, brother," he choked out.

Prince Amenhotep smiled as he said, "I will hunt you down in the afterlife. For as many times as needed, your spirit will be my prey!"

The brother slipped over the edge, pulling the prince with him. Both fell the great distance to the ground.

"No! No!" the high priestess wailed as she reached the edge. She looked down at their broken bodies. Coming to a decision, she pulled out the ankh and hit the lever. The blade, still dripping with the prince's blood, slid out.

"I will come back. I curse you, Amenhotep. I shall raise your brother and we shall rule for eternity!"

She began chanting. She plunged the dagger into her heart, falling over the edge to land with the prince and his brother.

I was startled to come back to reality. The students were still crying and screaming. Daniel was looking at me as if he would never see me again. Dad was still comforting Miral.

I looked up at the mummy and my vision began to blur. His rotting face morphed into that of Prince Amenhotep. All of his bandages fell away, and the remainder of his body looked as he had on the day he was married. His eyes smiled and my heart fluttered. My head felt funny, and I stepped back. In my place was Raia, smiling at her love.

The prince stood up and took Raia's hand in his. I handed them the scarab brooch as it glowed brighter and became even hotter.

"Thank you, Tamzin," the prince said.

"We are forever grateful," Raia said, directing her smile at me. She was radiant.

"We shall use the scarab."

I suddenly knew what was about to happen. And they would be gone forever.

"You can stay. Both of you. We would welcome you."

"No, dear Tamzin. We must set things right. We do not belong here," said the prince.

"Thank you for reuniting me with my love. I have been in misery without him."

"Yes. Thank you for freeing me. You have saved the both of us."

"We must leave. The afterlife awaits," Raia said, linking her arm with the prince's.

They both looked at the scarab as it became brighter and brighter. I turned my head and noticed that the stormy clouds were well above us—we would crash any second now.

The scarab became so bright that I couldn't see the couple anymore.

My gift to you, Tamzin. Live to save the world another day.

It was the prince's voice, but I still couldn't see him. Both he and Raia had disappeared into the light. The scarab was in midair for a moment, then dropped and cracked open. A huge surge of power shook the structure. It seemed almost sonic and my bones ached. We were all thrown to the ground as the museum slowed and came to a near halt as it lowered back into the earth and was still.

We ran outside and were greeted with the site of Springfield on the horizon. Prince Amenhotep had used the power of the scarab to give us a safe landing. The students were cheering, and I felt two strong arms encircle me. Daniel held tight and nibbled on my ear.

"See... piece of cake."

I turned around, punching him in the shoulder.

"Oh yeah, sure, piece of cake..." I said.

I saw Dad emerge with Miral. They both looked like they had been to hell and back. At least we were all still alive. Even the homeless looked happy to be down on solid ground.

I saw my mom in the distance and I ran over to her, giving her a hug. She had tears in her eyes. Wow, she almost never cried. She gently pushed me away and held me at arm's length.

She ran her thumb across my cheek. "My beautiful and strong daughter... I'm so proud of you. Since we made it through that, I think we can survive just about anything at this point."

I laughed. "I'm hoping we don't have to deal with anything like that ever again. I love you, Mom."

"Love you, too, Tam."

Dad and Miral ran over to us.

"Irene!" Dad grabbed my mom and gave her a tight hug. Tears were streaming down Mom's face, but I hadn't seen her look this happy in a long time.

After a few minutes, Miral tapped my dad's shoulder and cleared her throat. "May I cut in?" I was confused as to why she wanted to hug my dad since we were all just together, but I was even more surprised when Dad backed away and Miral pulled my mom in for a hug.

I looked at Dad, raising my eyebrows. He shrugged, chuckling to himself.

"Uhm... I thought you two hated each other," I said as they were pulling away from the embrace.

Mom wiped the tears from her cheeks and said, "Lapse in judgment due to the heat of the moment?"

Miral nodded in agreement. "Definitely, lapse in judgment."

Dad scoffed, making his way over to Mom and Miral, standing between them, putting one arm around each of their shoulders.

"I'll have you know, Tamzin, that these two ladies were best friends in college."

My eyes went wide in disbelief. "What? You're kidding."

"Nope, it's the truth. Both of them were madly in love with me and constantly fought because of it. Clearly, I was quite the catch back in the day."

Mom and Miral gave each other a look and they both rolled their eyes. Mom punched Dad in the shoulder, crossing her arms over her chest.

"Emphasis on the *was*," Miral said, punching Dad on the other shoulder.

"Hey!" Dad said, pretending to be upset.

I smiled, trying to picture the two of them as friends. It seemed like a stretch now, but I could almost see it working...

18

"To Tamzin!" Tony said, holding up his slice of pizza in a toast.

Macy, Jimmy, and I each held up our slices, Macy and Jimmy saying in unison, "To Tamzin!"

It was nice to finally be back with my friends after everything that had just happened. Tony and Macy were sitting next to each other on one side of the table and Jimmy and I were on the other. Things with Jimmy were still... well, I had no idea where we stood because we hadn't really talked since the concert, so we weren't sitting as close together as Tony and Macy were. I felt a little awkward. Even though I was happy to be back with everyone, I just felt out of place, out of the loop. So much had happened with them that I haven't really been around for.

"Tam, we gotta get you up to speed since you've been off saving the world and such," Tony said, taking a bite of his pizza.

"What have I missed?"

Tony looked at Macy, taking her hand and entwining it in his. He held their interlaced hands up above the table and Macy laughed.

I pointed between to the two of them. "You two? No, really? *No one* saw that coming." I shook my head at them.

Tony wiggled his eyebrows at me.

"We just thought you should know for sure," Macy said, looking at Tony. Her face scrunched up when she saw him wiggling his eyebrows and she said, "What are you doing with your face?"

"I could say the same to you, babe." He tapped her on the nose. "But hey, you're cute, so it's okay."

"Get a room, will ya?" I said, taking a bite of my slice of pizza. Jimmy had been relatively quiet the entire time, eating his food and listening. He still seemed to be enjoying himself, though. "Anything else I should know about?"

The three of them looked at each other as if they were checking to see if there was anything else that they had to tell me, and they all seemed to be at a loss. Jimmy suddenly sat up straighter, like he had thought of something. "We have another concert coming up," Jimmy said, face lighting up. He didn't look directly at me when he said it, but at least he was talking now.

"That's right!" Tony said, holding his hand out to give Jimmy a high five. "You guys killed it last time. I think we all had a great time."

Right as he was saying this, the bell on the door to the pizza place rang. I wouldn't have thought anything of it if Tony didn't start waving hysterically for the person to come over. I turned around and saw the last person I wanted to see. Vanessa strolled over to the table, pulling up a chair next to Jimmy.

"Hey, y'all. Fancy meeting you here," Vanessa said.

I was too shocked to be angry right now. I was *not* expecting to see her. Especially not so close to Jimmy, outside of their performances.

"Surprise! I invited Vanessa," Tony said, doing jazz hands. "I hope that's okay."

I forced a smile onto my face. Jimmy shifted in his seat, looking uncomfortable.

"I'm happy to see all of you guys," Vanessa said, looking directly at Jimmy.

"You going to get a slice of pizza?" Macy asked.

"I probably shouldn't... Dairy is bad for the vocals and all." I wanted to ask why she even came then, but held back. I didn't like her, but I didn't *hate* her. I wanted to stay civil.

"So, can we talk about that finale at the last performance?" she said, eyeing me. I guess *she* didn't want to be civil. "I know that Jimmy was more than happy with the way things turned out." She rubbed Jimmy's arm, smiling. Okay, I did hate her.

"I've had enough of this," I said, angrily pushing back my chair and walking toward the door to leave. I grabbed my purse, turning on my heels to get out of there as quickly as possible. I didn't even get to finish my pizza, but my appetite was gone. Right before I turned around to leave, I saw Macy give Tony a seething look.

"Tam, wait!" Jimmy said. I didn't even turn around. I walked right out the door.

I was heading down the sidewalk when I heard someone quickly approaching me from behind. I knew it was Jimmy before he said anything—I could pick out the sound of his footsteps in a heartbeat.

"Tam, please. Can you stop so we can talk about this?"

I kept walking. He had caught up to me and was walking next to me.

I refused to look at him, but I stopped. "What? There's nothing to talk about."

"Well, clearly there is if you're mad at me. You won't even look at me."

I rolled my eyes, crossing my arms over my chest. "You know why I'm mad."

"No, I really don't."

Why were all guys so *clueless*? "Honestly? You have no idea why I'm mad? Jimmy, you kissed her. Right in front of me!" I screamed, trying not to cry.

He opened his mouth then closed it, like he was trying to choose his words carefully. "Tam, I didn't kiss her. She kissed me. I wasn't expecting it. But either way, it was all just part of the act. It didn't mean anything. She doesn't mean anything to me."

He paused, inhaling, then let out a long sigh. "But that's not what this is really about, is it?" he asked quietly. "Vanessa kissing me was just your excuse. C'mon, Tam, you've been distant long before any of this happened. Just be straight up with me."

Tears stung my eyes. I've been so caught up with the fact that Jimmy and Vanessa kissed, I couldn't really think about anything else. Things with us have been fizzling out for a while now, but I hadn't wanted to admit it. "I don't know what to say, Jimmy. I don't know what you want to hear."

"This is not about what I want to hear. The only thing I want is for you to be honest with me. I'm probably not going to like it, but I can't deal with whatever this is anymore," he said, pointing between the two of us. "I've been dealing with a lot of shit, too. But I get that your adventures in saving the world clearly outweigh everyone else's problems." Jimmy joked around a lot, but I had never heard him sound so sarcastic or bitter.

"Hold on right there. That is so not fair. I care Jimmy! I never stopped caring. I'm sorry that I've been busy, but that doesn't mean I'm not concerned about what's going on with you. I haven't heard from you once in the past few days. It seems to me like you're the one who doesn't care anymore." I cringed when I said that. Sure, that thought had crossed my mind, but I had never voiced such a drastic accusation out loud.

He looked at me and staggered backward as if I had just physically hit him. I saw a single tear roll down his cheek.

"How dare you accuse me of not caring. Everything that I've done, I've done for you, for my friends, for my family. Nothing in my life, *nothing*, has ever been about me. Even music isn't something that is entirely mine! And what can I call mine if I don't even have music?" He clenched and unclenched his fists at his sides. "The real reason I got into playing was because when I was younger, I saw old pictures of my dad in a band. I didn't care that he walked out on the family—I still wanted to feel some sort of connection. Even now, when I'm up there on stage, I look out into the crowd, at all the different faces. I'm always wondering, *hoping*, that one of them will be my dad."

I wasn't sure how to respond, so I tried to put into words how I've been feeling.

"I'm not the same person, Jimmy. I'm not *your* Tam anymore. I'm different, and I'm just finally realizing that. I want different things, and I don't know if you can offer them to me."

He looked at me, several emotions crossing his face—the most prominent being pain... unadulterated pain—before his expression went blank.

"Are you saying what I think you're saying?" he asked, clenching his fists again.

"Jimmy, I don't think it would be fair to you if we stayed together. I think we should break up," I said, the words rushing out of my mouth in one breath.

He blinked twice, then gave me a curt nod. "Okay, then. Bye, Tamzin."

I opened my mouth to say something, but he had already turned around and started walking away from me. I watched him leave, tears stinging my eyes.

He stopped, shoulders going rigid. Without turning around, he said, "Oh, by the way. That stuff I said I was dealing with that you never asked about? Well, my mom's MS has gotten even worse and the doctors said she only has a few months left to live."

I held the tears in until he was out of my field of vision. I sank to the ground, sobbing as my shoulders shook violently.

What have I done?

~

I locked myself in my room. Mom tried to bring some food up for me, but I had no appetite. I was just lying in bed, staring at the ceiling and trying not to cry.

Sure, I was the one that wanted this, but that doesn't mean that it didn't hurt any less.

I felt like absolute crap. Jimmy was such an amazing guy, and he didn't deserve to be treated like this. I know for a fact that I hurt him, and it wasn't like I was nice when we were talking. During the entirety of our relationship, I had never seen him so stressed or angry.

I felt stupid lying here, feeling sorry for myself. In a way, this is what I went through after I lost Vickie. I knew that Jimmy hadn't been killed like Vickie had, he was very much alive thank God, but it still felt like he was taken away from me—though, it was my choice this time. I just wasn't expecting all of this to be so messy. Of course, I wasn't expecting unicorns and rainbows either, but definitely not *this*.

I needed something to cheer me up, something to distract me...

Just as I was thinking this, I heard something move next to me. My eyes quickly opened, and I shot up in bed, looking in the direction of the sound. I almost jumped out of my skin when I saw Daniel standing next to my dresser, moving to touch Beans.

"You rang?" he asked, smiling at me. His smile fell when he got a good look at my face. Great, I probably looked awful. "Oh, I hope I didn't scare you. Have you been crying?" He sat down next to me on the bed, slowly moving to wipe a tear from my cheek. I didn't even realize I had been crying.

"Uhm, I guess so. Things haven't been so good with me lately," I said, laughing at how much of an understatement that was.

"Everyone's okay, though, right? Er, alive, that is?"

"Yeah, nothing like that happened, don't worry. I just mean my social life. I think that's just about dead now."

"What happened? If you don't mind me asking."

I considered lying to him, but I figured there was no reason. "Jimmy and I broke up," I said quietly, trying to keep my voice steady.

Daniel looked straight ahead, a serious expression on his face. "Oh..." He took a deep breath, sighing, then put his arm around me. "Tamzin, I'm so sorry. You didn't need this right now."

"But I did it!" I said, raising my voice. I realized that my mom might be able to hear me, so I tried to calm down. I didn't want her to know that Daniel was here. "I broke his heart, Daniel. I'm a terrible person. His life at home was crappy, and I just made everything that much worse." I ran my hands through my hair, shaking my head.

"You are not a terrible person. If you weren't entirely into the relationship, breaking up was probably for the best. Sure, you hurt him. But he'll get over it. You'll get over it. At least this way you're not stringing him along when you knew you weren't going to have a future with him."

"True. But I think you're very biased in this situation."

He pretended to be shocked, putting a hand over his chest. "Who, me? There is not even a hint of bias in my bones."

I tried to smile, but it felt more like a grimace.

He looked at me, studying my face. I couldn't make out his expression. It was like a mixture of happiness and sadness. Kind of like the look he gave me earlier—like I was something that he could never have.

He pulled me closer, wrapping his arm around my shoulders. He kissed the top of my head, resting his chin on my hair. The weight of everything that we weren't saying hung thick in the air.

"We need to find out what happened to you, Daniel." I was trying not to cry yet again, but I could feel the tears threatening.

"I know. I just can't remember anything."

"We need to see Nomi. Tomorrow. If something is going to go right, it is going to be us finding out who murdered you. You need closure."

"I hope that she can help."

"Me, too."

He looked at the clock on my dresser and slowly moved away to stand up. He pointed to my pillow, motioning for me to lie down. "It's getting late. You should get some sleep."

I was actually getting tired, so I moved my blankets aside, lying down. Daniel pulled the blankets over me, tucking me in and making sure I was properly covered. He bent down, his lips very lightly brushing mine, then he moved to turn off the light.

"Goodnight, Tam."

"Night, Daniel."

He smiled, turning away from me. He stood by the window, looking up at the moon.

"Oh, and Daniel?"

He turned around, raising his eyebrows.

"Thank you. Thank you for everything."

19

I met Daniel outside of Nomi's seance parlour. He gave me a hug and reached for my hand as we entered.

"Nomi? Nomi, are you here?"

She appeared through the beaded doorway. She almost looked panicked, which was the first time I had ever seen her lose her cool composure. Hugging me tightly, she said, "I'm sorry, Tamzin. I didn't mean for you to be transported there, body and all. When you disappeared, I thought I'd never see you again."

"It's okay, Nomi. Everything worked out."

"How is your father? I'm glad he is still alive."

"He's fine. He is staying at the hospital for a day because of dehydration. Plus, they wanted to keep an eye on him. A lot of the other victims are there, too."

"Geez, Girl, you are one formidable opponent of the dark forces! First, the demon Ripper and now an evil high priestess."

"Well, I had help." I nodded toward Daniel.

"This time, I nearly did the opposite when the priestess possessed me."

"Yes, but it worked out in the end." I squeezed his hand to reassure him. "And, without Daniel, we would never have destroyed the ankh."

"Yes. It took two supernatural beings and all their power," Nomi said.

"And Raia and Prince Amenhotep saved us from crashing to the ground. Teamwork all around."

I gave Daniel a quick kiss on the cheek. Nomi raised her eyebrow but didn't say anything.

"Nomi, we were wondering if you could try to read Daniel and see how he died? It's still a mystery, and we don't have any leads."

"Absolutely, my dear. Anything for your new *boyfriend*." She winked at me. "First, though, I want to give you a quick once over for any darkness that may have crept inside. Is that okay?"

"Sure, Nomi. Go right ahead."

She walked right up to me, face to face, and put her hands directly over my head. Closing her eyes, she slowly moved her hands down my body. She never touched me, but she was "feeling" my energy and aura. When she was done, she opened her eyes and smiled.

"Tam girl, your aura glows its natural light."

"Good to know."

This time, Daniel squeezed my hand.

"Let's go into the magic room to do your boy's reading."

We followed her through the beads into her psychic lair. Nomi sat across from Daniel.

"Let me see your hands."

She took his hand in hers.

"Please relax as this will help me with the reading."

Daniel's shoulders moved down a bit—I guess he had been tense.

"Okay. When I am in my trance state please do not let go of my hands. It will break the connection and we'll have to start again."

We both nodded. She closed her eyes and started swaying ever so slightly.

"Try to think of when you died. What happened by the river? Even if the memories are empty, push at that place in your subconscious. Poke and prod and reveal."

She swayed faster and started chanting under her breath. I could almost make out what she was saying—it sounded like Latin or Greek or something similar. She went on like this for a few minutes, then sat straight up.

"Who dares to see me!" she said in a low-pitched, gravelly voice. I jumped, but Daniel stayed firmly in place.

Her eyes flew open—they were entirely white!

"You cannot see me!" she shouted.

"Nomi? Are you okay?" I asked, eyes going wide.

"If you attempt to breach the sacred pact, you will be killed!"

She suddenly flew backward into the air and was pinned to the top of the wall near the ceiling. Daniel and I grabbed her and pulled her back to the ground.

"Nomi, are you there? Are you hurt?"

She shook her head and carefully stood up. Her eyes rolled back to normal.

"I will have a bruise, but nothing that some aspirin can't handle."

"Good. What the hell was that?" I asked.

"Something I have never been in contact with before. It was a dark, malevolent, ancient being. Very dangerous."

She began rummaging through one of her shelves of knick knacks. She found a necklace and handed it to me.

"Tamzin, you must wear this until you solve the mystery of Daniel's death."

I glanced down at it—it looked like a knight from a chess board. The part that went around my neck was a thin strip of leather.

"Girl, this is a protection amulet. That creature has power. More power than I've encountered in centuries."

Centuries?, I thought. I realized that now wasn't the time to ask how old Nomi was.

"I'll wear it."

"So, Nomi, did you get anything on what might have happened to me?" Daniel asked, a hint of hesitation creeping into his voice.

"The creature blocked me. I was about to see through the magic, but it slapped me away. Dark, dark magics at play here."

I was disappointed, but at least now we knew why Daniel couldn't remember anything. This all powerful entity wanted it to be kept secret.

"Sorry, Nomi, for this trouble. Thank you for helping, though."

"I am always here for you, Tamzin. Please be careful."

"We will."

I gave her a hug and we turned to leave.

~

146

I had on my pajamas and was getting ready for bed. Nomi's necklace was around my neck. I rubbed my fingers up and down over its smooth surface. I was definitely not going to take it off after what happened. I picked up Beans and tucked him into bed next to me. I didn't really feel like sleeping alone tonight. Right after his head hit the pillow, I heard the "*Zzzz...*" in my head. Since it was so quiet, it actually helped me sleep. I drifted off, hoping not to have any nightmares.

I was awoken by a frenzied Beans. It took everything I had in me not to scream when I heard his voice.

"Tamzin! Tamzin!"

"Beans?"

"It is here! It is here!"

"What's here?"

"The bad thing."

"It's okay Beans... You were just having a nightmare."

"No, no. Bad thing here."

As always, communicating with Beans was difficult at best. I guess he did help me realize my dad was in trouble, though.

"Can you tell me what the bad thing is?"

"No. Dead monkey won't let me. He is mean!"

"What does the bad thing do?"

"It... It does bad things!"

"I don't understand, Beans."

"Here. I can show. Pick me up."

I picked him up, holding him close. His cheek came into contact with mine.

I was standing on the top floor of a near-empty parking garage. I saw a young couple by the edge and walked over to them. They were holding hands, looking out over the cityscape. We were in a major metropolis and many people were moving around quickly below on the street.

The couple turned to kiss, and I had the distinct impression that I knew the girl. I saw her dark hair and button nose and realized that it was Max—it had to be. Only here, she was in her early twenties. She was clearly in love with the guy she was with. It was weird but

147

also nice to see her grown up, looking like she was happy and healthy. I wondered if she still danced...

The couple turned and walked toward me, then walked right through me. I guess this was more like the astral projection that Nomi had attempted earlier. There was a loud whine in the air. Maxie and her beau turned back to me and looked up at the sky. I didn't see anything, but whatever was making the noise had everyone's attention.

Looking off in the distance, I made out a trail of white smoke, like from a jet when it flew overhead. The trail came down in the middle of the city. A massive explosion rang out, followed by a mushroom cloud. It was a bomb!

The cloud plumed up into the sky as a massive shockwave emanated outward, turning buildings to dust. One by one, the buildings fell. I looked at the people down the street. As the wave hit them, they were vaporized into smoke. The blast took out the building across the street.

I turned back around and Max and the boy were holding onto each other tightly. As it hit them, everything seemed to happen in slow motion. Layers of Maxie's skin peeled away, revealing muscle and sinew. The muscle and sinew evaporated, leaving only bone. The bones held out for a split second longer, only to be vaporized, leaving nothing.

I was jolted back to the safety of my room, shaking from head to toe.

"See! Bad thing here!" Beans said.

"Beans, how does that vision relate to something here?"

"I... I... I can't say. Dead monkey won't let me."

"Where is this bad thing?"

"Downstairs."

"Okay, let's go see it."

"No, no! We need to leave!"

"Beans, we have to figure it out. I saw my young friend Max in the vision. She was much older, so it won't happen for many more years."

"Please, please don't."

"It's okay, Beans."

"I guess. But, don't touch it!"

"I won't."

I carried him downstairs and we looked around. The kitchen light was on, so I wondered if Dad was back from the hospital. Neither of my parents liked hospitals, so they made their stays as short as possible.

Heading down to the *Dungeon of Curious Oddities*, I noticed that the lights were on here, too. Yep, my dad must have gotten home. I went over to the unboxing table and found what looked like an ancient box with mystical symbols on it.

"Is that what you're talking about, Beans?"

"No, no, no."

"Is it okay if I open the box?"

"I don't know."

Throwing caution to the wind, I grabbed a pencil and flipped the lid open. I nearly fainted as I stepped back. It was the Monkey Paw! I had always had nightmares when I was younger about this thing. And now it was sitting right in front of me.

"Bad thing! Bad thing!"

"I know, Beans. I won't touch it."

"Tamzin."

"Yes, Beans?"

"Must tell you."

"What?"

"Dead monkey will be mad."

"It's okay, Beans. I will protect you."

For some reason, I could sense the strength he was mustering up to tell me—strength mixed with sadness. He pushed and pushed until I thought he was going to burst. I held him, looking right into his eyes as he said:

"I killed Daniel!"

Coming Soon!
Tamzin Clarke v the Monkey Paw

More of Lauren's books on Amazon

Lauren's Facebook page

Lauren's Goodreads Page

If you enjoyed Tamzin Clarke v the Mummy, we hope you will write a review. It may not seem like much, but they really help and we truly appreciate them.

www.ingramcontent.com/pod-product-compliance
Lightning Source LLC
Chambersburg PA
CBHW021109130626
46554CB00002B/609